What would it be like to make love to a man like Jake?

Even as an eighteen-year-old, Jake Cochran would have been gentle.

A loud bang startled Cassidy and interrupted her thoughts. She sat up with a gasp, the blanket falling to the floor, her heart pumping wildly.

Had someone banged on the door? Had someone found them? Had she seen the doorknob turn?

Rushing to the window, she peered through the darkness toward the lake. She had just about convinced herself she'd dreamed the noise when the face of a man appeared, wild-eyed, two inches from the windowpane.

Cassidy screamed and ran out into the hall. And encountered Jake.

A very wet, very naked Jake.

Dear Harlequin Intrigue Reader,

We have another great selection of exciting Harlequin Intrigue titles for you this month, kicking off with the second book in Rebecca York's 43 LIGHT STREET trilogy MINE TO KEEP. *Never Alone* is a very special story about the power of love and the lengths to which a man and woman will go to find each other—no matter the obstacles.

One down—three to go! Our MONTANA CONFIDENTIAL series continues with *Special Assignment: Baby* by Debra Webb. A covert operation and a cuddly baby are just a day's work for this sexy cowboy agent. And Caroline Burnes scorches the sheets in *Midnight Burning,* a story about one man's curse and his quest for redemption.

Finally, come play HIDE AND SEEK with Susan Kearney as she launches her new three-book miniseries with *The Hidden Years.*

So pick up all four for a dynamic reading experience.

Sincerely,

Denise O'Sullivan
Associate Senior Editor
Harlequin Intrigue

P.S. Next month Harlequin Intrigue proudly welcomes back Anne Stuart and Gayle Wilson in *Night and Day,* an extraordinary 2-in-1 keeper!

THE HIDDEN YEARS
SUSAN KEARNEY

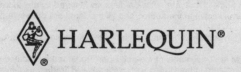

HARLEQUIN®

TORONTO • NEW YORK • LONDON
AMSTERDAM • PARIS • SYDNEY • HAMBURG
STOCKHOLM • ATHENS • TOKYO • MILAN • MADRID
PRAGUE • WARSAW • BUDAPEST • AUCKLAND

ISBN 0-373-22636-5

THE HIDDEN YEARS

Printed in U.S.A.

ABOUT THE AUTHOR

Susan Kearney used to set herself on fire four times a day; now she does something really hot—she writes romantic suspense. While she no longer performs her signature fire dive, (she's taken up figure skating), she never runs out of ideas for characters and plots. A business graduate from the University of Michigan, Susan writes full-time. She resides in a small town outside Tampa, Florida, with her husband and children and a spoiled Boston terrier. Visit her Web site at www.SusanKearney.com.

Don't miss any of our special offers. Write to us at the following address for information on our newest releases.

Harlequin Reader Service
U.S.: 3010 Walden Ave., P.O. Box 1325, Buffalo, NY 14269
Canadian: P.O. Box 609, Fort Erie, Ont. L2A 5X3

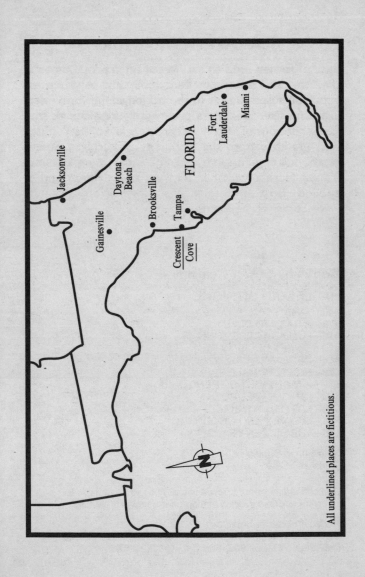

Jacksonville

Daytona
Beach

Gainesville

Brooksville

Tampa

FLORIDA

Crescent
Cove

Fort
Lauderdale

Miami

All underlined places are fictitious.

CAST OF CHARACTERS

Jake Cochran—As a child Jake made a promise to his father to keep the family together. But the state separated the children. Now nothing and no one can stop him from bringing the family together—not even Cassidy Atkins.

Cassidy Atkins—A lawyer who likes to live day-to-day. But Jake has other plans for her future.

Frazier Atkins—Cassidy's deceased father, who left behind secrets that can destroy his daughter.

Harrison Gordon—Jake's number-one employee and a crackerjack P.I.

Donna Rodale—Friend or foe? She's the mystery woman who can fill in the missing pieces of the puzzle. But first Jake and Cassidy must find her.

Burak Sansal—A spy. A double agent. Can he be trusted?

Ari Ben Goldstein—A former Israeli Mossad agent. He knew Jake's parents, but is he part of the problem or the solution?

For Gayle and Steve Brooks,
my favorite Brooksville relatives.

Chapter One

What the hell was she doing in Half Moon Bay? In his driveway?

Jake Cochran stared at the monitor that exhibited his front gate, a convertible driving through, a woman behind the wheel.

Cassidy Atkins.

It might have been ten years since he'd seen her last, but he hadn't forgotten that tawny skin or the lion's mane of multicolored gold that framed her face. It might have been more than a decade, but a warm glow of happiness started in his gut and radiated outward before he bottled it up. Ten years hadn't quite banished memories of the pain she'd caused.

Jake was no longer that vulnerable kid, but he could no more resist staring at Cassidy now than he could a decade ago. As she parked her red convertible, he hit a camera switch to zoom in on her. Cassidy smoothed her shoulder-length hair into a ponytail, freshened her lipstick and reached for her compact. Then, with an impatient gesture, she tucked the unused compact back into her purse.

Interesting. So he rated lipstick but not blush. A

visit but no warning phone call. Apparently Cassidy's impulsive and spontaneous nature hadn't changed over the years.

Cassidy gracefully exited the car, reached into the back seat and removed a box. Hip-hugging jeans encased her long legs and rounded hips. A crop top showed a smudge or two of dust as if she'd been working and impulsively decided to stop and pay him a visit. The girl he remembered might be unpredictable, but she usually had good reasons for her actions. And Jake guessed she hadn't phoned first because she was afraid he might refuse to see her.

Was she in some kind of trouble and in need of his help?

He frowned in puzzlement as Cassidy carried the carton toward his front door. It didn't take his detective skills to figure out that the reason behind her visit might be somehow connected to the box's contents. However, she couldn't be returning something he'd left behind, since ten years ago he hadn't owned enough possessions to fill that box. Back then, just out of high school and a state orphanage, he'd barely had a change of clothes. Yet his limited circumstances hadn't stopped him from foolishly dreaming of a future with Cassidy.

Jake had found out soon enough that Cassidy's father, Frazier Atkins, had bigger plans for his daughter than a relationship with Jake Cochran. Frazier's high expectations for his daughter included college, law school and eventually a husband from the same upper middle-class background as her own. And according to her father's plan, she was now well on her way to success. With only twenty miles between their respective homes on Florida's Gulf coast, Jake occasionally caught news of Cassidy and knew she'd earned her law degree and set up practice with her father in Crescent Cove.

Jake angled the camera lens onto her left hand. Ha! No wedding ring. Another zing of pleasure sneaked over him before he flicked off the camera and headed downstairs to meet the girl he'd never been able to forget.

Before she rang the bell, he opened the door and caught the breathless look of surprise in widened eyes still as blue as Tampa's sky. But not quite as joyous and exuberant as he remembered. These blue eyes couldn't quite hold his gaze and reflected a bit of indecision, along with a sophistication that quickly covered the flash of uncertainty he'd first glimpsed.

Nevertheless he enjoyed drinking in the sight of her upturned face, which glowed with a healthy tan. He lingered over the straight nose, the delicately arched brows, the heart-shaped cheeks that she'd always wished were high and sharp like a model's, instead of impishly round, matching her personality.

"Hi, Sunshine." He used his old pet name for her without thinking, his voice slightly huskier than he would have liked.

Cassidy's full lips turned up in a crooked smile, but uncertainty again flickered in her eyes. "Jake."

He opened the door, feeling a measure of both pleasure and wariness at seeing her again but mostly wondering what caused the shadows in her eyes. "Come in."

She took in the trappings of his success—the soaring ceiling of his foyer, the marble floors and designer wallpaper—without the least bit of surprise. Almost as if she'd expected his prosperity. Had she kept track of him? Jake thought not. Why would she?

Obviously worried, she clutched that box so hard her fingernails dug into the cardboard and left tiny crescent indentations. Over the years Jake had become good at reading strangers who came to his detective agency seeking his help. His experience as a detective told him she had something unpleasant to tell him. His experience as a man told him this was a nervous woman.

Yet Jake wasn't just operating with his powers of observation or by instinct alone. Cassidy was no stranger. Impulsive, spontaneous, giving, she liked to go with the flow, live day to day. She kept her long-term goals in sight, but her free-spirited nature ruled her most of the time. This wasn't one of those times. Today she was serious. She had a way of angling her chin whenever she was uncertain. She had it tipped at that angle now as she glanced at him.

He led her past his office into the room that overlooked Tampa Bay. Perhaps the soft cries of gulls and the salty breeze would soothe her nerves. Gingerly she placed the box on the glass table as if fearing it would break, then dusted off her hands.

"Can I get you something to drink?" he offered as he gestured to a chair for her to have a seat. "Iced tea? Water? A cola?"

"No, thanks."

Jake waited. He'd learned to be patient, learned that when someone wanted to tell him something, it was usually best to let them come to it in their own way.

Cassidy took in a deep breath of air, then let it out

slowly and rolled her shoulders. Slowly she raised those sea-blue eyes to his. "My father died last year."

"I heard. And I'm sorry. For your sake."

He folded his arms over his chest, refusing to be hypocritical. He'd never liked Frazier Atkins. Ten years ago Jake had known the man disapproved of him, a boy with no family. No past. And probably not much of a future. But Jake had succeeded, throwing his efforts into his detective agency with a determination that had left no room for failure.

While Jake might have found security, he suspected mere financial success wouldn't have been enough for Frazier Atkins. The prominent attorney had wanted a better match for his only daughter than a kid from the wrong side of town. While Jake had acquired a veneer of sophistication along the way to success, he lacked the Old World charm that took several generations to acquire. Quite simply, in Frazier's eyes, Jake could never have been good enough to even wipe the dirt off Cassidy's sneakers. And he'd coolly made his point to his daughter—not by arguing, but by fighting a battle Jake couldn't win. Frazier had sent her out West to college. He'd put a distance between them that a boy with barely enough funds to feed himself couldn't overcome.

He'd always hoped Cassidy would call, visit him during spring break, but it hadn't happened. She'd accepted her father's wishes and hadn't looked back.

And through his scheming, Frazier had remained polite, cool and secretive toward Jake. But Jake had always suspected that Cassidy's father had known more about Jake's past than he'd been willing to admit. Yet Jake had no more been able to prove that the wily attorney had been holding out on him than he had been able to prove to Cassidy that her father had sent her away to separate her from the wrong kind of boy.

Cassidy pushed the box toward Jake. "I took over Dad's law practice and found this."

"What is it?" Jake made no move to open the box. Instead, he sat and watched Cassidy swallow hard, wet her top lip and try to hold his eyes.

Opening the box with shaking fingers, she looked from the papers inside back to him, her eyes dark and mysterious. "You ever find your sisters?"

Her question rocked him to the core. He'd unconsciously figured that Cassidy had come here seeking his help. He hadn't expected the conversation to revolve around him. Or his sisters.

His sisters.

Jake shook his head at the failure that still haunted his nightmares. Nightmares of a five-year-old child promising his father that he'd help look after the family. That he'd watch over his sisters. Keep the family together. His mother had died overseas, and a week later his father had brought the family back to the U.S., where he'd been killed in a car accident. Awake, Jake couldn't recall exactly what had happened to his sisters. In the darkest of dreams, shadowy creatures with no faces pulled the kicking and screaming girls from his arms. Every few months Jake still awoke in a sweat, heart pounding, choking on tears.

He glanced at the box, curiosity welling up. "I always thought your father was keeping back information on my sisters' locations. Was he?"

Her expression grim, Cassidy nodded. "He knew more than he revealed."

"They're alive?"

Again Cassidy nodded.

Son of a bitch! Jake stood so fast that his chair crashed to the floor. If Frazier Atkins had stood before him now, it would have taken all of Jake's considerable control not to strike him.

Jake paced, fuming. "Your old man could have saved me ten years of searching. Ten years of not knowing whether my sisters had lived or died. Ten years of waking up every morning and going to sleep every night wondering if I had any family left or if I was all alone in the world."

"I'm sorry, Jake. My father never told me the truth, either."

Although Jake had never found his sisters, he'd never given up searching. Would never give up. But he had no more to go on now than he'd had ten years ago, when the day after he'd graduated from high school, he'd looked up Frazier Atkins. Jake had hoped the attorney who'd handled his custody arrangements could help find his sisters. But Cassidy's father had stubbornly refused to tell him anything.

Jake paced, needing an outlet for his anger. Frazier had deliberately kept him apart from his sisters. How dare he separate a family? Jake wanted to strike out and hit something to relieve his frustration. But long ago he'd learned to master his anger, and within moments, he'd replaced burning rage with simmering control. Reaching down, he lifted the chair and replaced it exactly where it had been.

Cassidy's voice pleaded with him. "You have to

understand. A lawyer's first obligation is to his client."

"And just who was the client?" Jake asked, folding his arms over his chest and watching Cassidy closely.

"I'm not...sure."

"Let me get this straight. Frazier Atkins couldn't tell me how to find my sisters because..."

"Because the custody matters were sealed. Ditto for the adoption records, unless both parties ask for the records."

"You're saying my sisters were adopted?"

"Yes."

"They're together?"

As she heard the concern he couldn't mask, Cassidy shook her head, regret in her gaze. "I don't believe so." A tremor of distress tinged her voice. "The records indicate that all three of you were split up."

Jake frowned hard. He knew that the state generally tried to keep siblings together. Maybe he'd been an ornery little boy that no one wanted—too old to interest a family, too old for parents to love, and so he'd never been adopted. Couples came to the orphanage seeking toddlers and babies. But his sisters had been young.

"Surely it wouldn't have been that difficult to keep two little girls together."

Cassidy seemed to gather her wits and spoke with authority. "The entire adoption proceedings were very unusual. Names were changed. The girls were sent to different parts of the state before families were found for them."

"Why?"

Cassidy shrugged and this time a hint of darkness clouded her eyes. "I don't know. I haven't gone through the box's contents that carefully. As soon as I saw that—"

"Your father's silence has kept a family apart."

"—you would be interested, I just drove over."

So coming here had been an impulsive act. He'd been right that her spontaneous nature hadn't changed, but it gave him no satisfaction. Too many memories spun through his mind. Frazier Atkins and his damn secrets. Cassidy and what she'd once meant to Jake. All the memories in murky shadows, except his one bright hope that someday he could fulfill his childhood promise to his father. Find his sisters. Bring them together again. Only then would he be free to start a family of his own.

"I thought I could help you track down your sisters from these old addresses," Cassidy said as she turned to the box and began to open it.

"Why?" Jake snapped the question as hard and fast as the crack of a whip.

At his tone, Cassidy jumped as if he'd slapped her hand away from the box. Her eyes flashed with guilt and heat. "I feel bad that my father never gave you..." Her hand fluttered over the box.

He stared at her, fascinated by the changing hue in her eyes, by the tightening of her lips and the questioning arch of her brows. And fury filled his soul, fury that she thought she could just prance back into his life, insert herself into his thoughts. Invade his privacy. Witness his pain and failure.

"I don't need your help," he told her without bothering to keep the bitterness from his voice.

"You're angry?"

Anger wasn't the right word for what he felt right now. Rage, white-hot rage, cascaded through him, rage at not just Frazier Atkins, but at the injustice done to a child who still carried a man-size guilt.

He'd failed to find his sisters. He'd promised his father. And failed.

Frazier Atkins's silence had kept him at a dead end for ten years. But he'd never stopped searching. He'd wasted hours, days, months, years. All because of Frazier Atkins.

As rage rose up to mock him, Jake knew he was close to losing control. And he didn't want Cassidy to know how badly her father had hurt him. Didn't want her to know how much she could still disturb him by being here and witnessing his pain.

He kept his voice cool and clipped. "I think you'd better go."

Her eyes shimmered with sadness and determination. "But I want to help."

"Your family has *helped* me enough," he sneered, and watched her face go pale.

Raising her chin, she squared her shoulders and met his gaze with a level one of her own. "You're not being fair."

"Like your father was fair to me? By hiding my sisters' location from their only brother?"

Exasperation tinged her tone. "I already explained. A lawyer's first obligation is to his client."

"Yeah, right. A nonexistent client."

She nodded coolly, as if giving him a point in a debate. "I can't find the record of who hired him. He was paid in cash."

"How convenient."

Jake ached to clench his fists. He didn't, fearing if he did he might follow through and punch the wall. Instead, he forced his tone to remain crisp and precise. "And maybe, just like your father, you're keeping the truth from me now. Maybe you know exactly who hired your father to split up my family."

She flinched. If he hadn't been a sizzling mass of emotions and so eager for her to go before she could witness his pain, he'd have admired the gumption it took for her to look him in the eye. But right now, all her courage did was feed the flames of his rage and resentment.

Cassidy locked gazes with him, as if she expected him to read her sincerity. "I'd like to make up for what my father did."

Her concern only stoked his anger. He didn't want her help, her pity or her compassion. He couldn't bear for her to know how much her father's silence had hurt him. And he was too proud to tell her how hurt he'd been when she'd left for college and never once called him. Or how just her presence flayed open old scars and brought the hurting back.

Jake needed to be alone, needed time to lick his wounds. "This isn't your concern."

"I was concerned enough to bring you the box."

"So you salved your conscience, Sunshine."

"Don't call me that."

Ah. The nickname had memories for her, too. Had he struck a nerve?

Long ago Jake had learned to fight the world with the tools he'd been given—a quick mind and a ruth-lessness that was revealed whenever he felt under attack, his back to the wall. He needed time to think, time to recover from the raw emotions churning his gut, and he sure as hell didn't need Cassidy here.

He allowed an edge of rage to penetrate his tone. "Go back to your safe little lawyer's world. The world your daddy picked for you. He's probably rolling over in his grave right now." Jake scowled at her. "We both know Frazier wouldn't have wanted you here with me."

At his hurtful words, she raised her chin and softened her tone, but steel braced her spine. "What do *you* want?"

He couldn't let those eyes see into his heart, see the scars he'd have sworn had healed until she walked through the door. He didn't want the memories that sliced through him. He didn't want to remember what it was like to want her.

Never again would he let her fool him into believing she cared about him. He was no longer an innocent boy just out of a state home, but a grown man who'd seen enough betrayal and deceit to know the world could be ugly.

When she didn't budge, he made his voice glacial. "I don't want your help. I don't want you in my home. I don't want *you*. Is that clear enough? Blunt enough?"

Cassidy's pale face turned whiter, leaving blotchy red patches of anger and humiliation on her cheeks. Her lips narrowed, their fullness pulled into a taut line of distress. As she stood, she didn't say a word. With surprising strength, she lifted the box, turned it upside down and dumped the contents onto the floor at his feet.

Papers, a diary and photographs spilled into a messy pile. Jake ignored the papers and watched Cassidy, finally realizing he'd gone too far. But he couldn't find the words to say so. Too many conflicting emotions made his mouth dry, and words of apology stuck in his throat.

With her head high, her shoulders back, her chin up, her spine ramrod straight, Cassidy strode from the room with the empty carton. And although Jake had gotten exactly what he'd intended, he felt no triumph. She'd left him with an empty house and an empty heart.

Cassidy would not sob. Not here where he might see her. So she held her breath all the way out of Jake's house and down the walk. She didn't dare inhale until she reached her car. Finally as tears tightened the back of her throat, she took air into her starving lungs in one big rush.

She would not cry for the boy she'd once called a friend. She would not spill tears over the harsh man who'd replaced him. She would not think about the reasons that caused the confident young friend she recalled to turn into the cynical man she'd seen today.

She would not cry.

No, you'll just run away, her conscience needled her.

He told me to leave so he could brood in private.

He was your best friend. A good friend. How could you leave such an intriguing hunk alone when there are so many other possibilities?

He was like a big brother.

Didn't you ever think of consoling him? All that wonderful anger could be put to good use.

Sure. I'll just sprinkle fairy dust over him and he'll turn from an old friend into the perfect lover.

I see you prefer crying.

I'm not crying.

Cassidy tossed the box into the car and angrily wiped away the solitary tear running from the corner of her eye.

That Jake had grown into such a handsome man hadn't surprised her. She'd always admired his whiskey-colored eyes, olive skin and black hair. But during the past ten years, he'd grown another few inches, towering over her five foot eight, and his features had sharpened. The hollows under his cheekbones had grown deeper. His eyes glittered with an intensity that almost made her shiver. The changes in his eyes bothered her the most. Eyes that she recalled as warm and friendly as a puppy's now burned with amber fire. Even outside in the breezy Gulf air, she could still recall their blazing heat.

However, she would not think about the pain of betrayal she'd seen in his eyes when she'd told him that her father had had the answers that he'd so desperately sought. If only her father were still alive so he could explain his actions. Despite what Jake thought, she knew her father had been a good man. He must have had an honorable reason for his seemingly inexplicable actions.

Cassidy had never told Jake that her father had insisted that she follow her dream of college and law school and had discouraged her from considering Jake as anything more than a friend. Jake would have assumed that his poor background and lack of family and education were the reason Frazier had insisted that his daughter attend college as she'd always planned. And Cassidy couldn't hurt Jake with something he'd had no control over.

Even at eighteen she'd understood why her father wanted her to follow her dream of becoming a lawyer and not give up like Cassidy's mother had. Her parents had married during law school. After her mother had become pregnant, she'd dropped out of school, and while she'd always intended to return, she never had. Her mother had put her dream on hold—and then she'd died. And her father insisted that Cassidy put her education first.

So she hadn't let herself become involved with Jake for the sake of a dream. Cassidy's goal was to practice law. Jake's dream was to have a family. To him family meant everything—especially since he'd never had one. And he never ever took relationships casually, because he'd had so few people who'd cared about him. Because Cassidy didn't trust herself with Jake, because she couldn't let their friendship change, she'd deliberately chosen to stop any further feelings from developing between them.

She'd always looked at Jake as a brother, and they'd kept that platonic friendship until she'd left for college.

When a slip of paper that hadn't fallen from the box earlier wafted into the air on a gust, Cassidy snatched the paper by instinct and crushed it. She didn't care if that paper had the names, addresses and social-security numbers of both of Jake's sisters. No way would she return to that house. She couldn't face another of Jake's rebuffs.

He'd made it very clear that she wasn't wanted, and Cassidy wouldn't stay and help now if he came out on his knees and begged. That image brought a slight upward quirk to her lips. The thought of Jake Cochran begging anyone was a ludicrous image.

A bit calmer, Cassidy slipped behind the steering wheel, the paper still crumpled in her fingers. She backed out of the drive, letting the wheels squeal as she turned a sharp corner, eager to leave behind the disturbing image of an angry Jake. But she couldn't relax the tension in her shoulders even after she passed out of sight of Jake's house.

What had happened to him? She mourned the loss of the young man she'd known, recalling their short time together with a fondness that couldn't have been totally one-sided. They'd been good friends, sharing their dreams and hopes for the future. She'd told Jake how she wanted to follow in her father's footsteps and become a lawyer. He'd spoken of finding his family and joining Special Forces. They'd rarely argued, and she recalled a unique closeness. She'd thought of him as the older brother she'd always wanted and never had. Or were her memories skewed? She'd always believed Jake had liked her. But maybe he'd just used her friendship in an attempt to get to her father. If that had been his plan, he'd failed. To her knowledge, her father had never spoken to anyone about the adoptions. Not even to her.

Remembering she needed to pick up a few things, Cassidy stopped for gas and bought fresh milk at the convenience store. She ran the car through the wash and checked the tires for air before slipping back behind the wheel. She headed for home, determined to ignore Jake and his problems.

Cassidy stopped at a red light and started to toss the crumpled paper she'd left on the seat into the trash. But she noticed writing on the paper and looked more carefully. Numbers. A ten-digit phone number.

Curious, Cassidy punched the numbers into her car phone. As the light turned green, a bored-sounding female voice answered. "Password, please."

Password?

Behind Cassidy, a car honked. "Hold on a sec."

She pulled off the road and parked, then stared at the yellowed slip of paper while the bored voice requested again, "Password, please."

Cassidy flipped over the paper and read the scrawled script aloud, "Blow back?"

She heard several clicks and then a different voice said, "One moment."

Pleased with herself, Cassidy waited, wondering who would answer the other end of the line. She waited at least a minute or two and was about to hang up when a harried male voice finally responded. "Who are you working for? How did you get this number?"

Suddenly nervous as the voice demanded answers, Cassidy speculated about whom she was talking with and why he was acting as if she'd done something illegal. "I'm sorry, I must have the wrong number."

Quickly she hung up the phone and then tossed the paper into her purse. She wouldn't return to give it to Jake, but maybe she'd mail it. Then she remembered how he'd treated her. Maybe she wouldn't bother.

Cassidy drove into Crescent Cove along sunny palm-lined streets, and slowly the tension left her shoulders. Her grip on the steering wheel eased. Her hometown usually had a relaxing effect on her. In Crescent Cove, the neighbors still knew one another and waved as Cassidy drove by. The kid next door mowed the lawn and children played in the yards and laughed on swing sets. If the state hadn't been undergoing a drought and the county hadn't been under water restrictions, the kids would be running under sprinklers. Instead, they made do with bikes and in-line skates.

Her own lawn was turning brown, but tomorrow was her morning to water. Cassidy used the automatic opener and pulled in to her two-car garage, then closed the door behind her. Glad to be home in the house she'd inherited from her father, along with his small-town law practice, Cassidy opened the door that led into the kitchen she loved. The oak table she'd found at the flea market last month still needed another coat of varnish, but she was pleased by the effect it made under the curtains decorated with daisies.

A trash can lay on its side.

Cassidy straightened the can with a frown. Had another duck flown down the chimney? Cautiously she headed into the den and set her purse on the table. The morning sun usually shone brightly through the window, but she must have forgotten to open the curtains.

After her father died, she'd redecorated, painting the plastered walls a yellow that complemented the gleaming parquet floors. She'd bought colorful seascapes by local artists and added a homey touch to the couch with hand-embroidered pillows. Cassidy spoiled herself by buying fresh flowers every week. She'd picked sprigs of orange blossoms off her citrus tree out back, and the scents mingled in a flowery bouquet. She sniffed appreciatively and caught a whiff of smoke. With the drought conditions, everyone feared fires.

But this smelled like cigarette smoke.

The hair on the back of Cassidy's neck stirred. Had someone been in the house? The next thought felt like a punch to her stomach. Suppose she wasn't alone.

Cassidy didn't hesitate. She whirled on her heel to head back toward the kitchen.

The curtain in the den moved. Was someone behind it? Or had a breeze caught it, flickering ominous shadows across the wood floor?

Cassidy changed direction. Heard a footstep that wasn't hers. A thud.

Heart pumping, she raced down the hall toward the front door. Lost time twisting the dead bolt. Flung open the door.

A hand clamped down on her shoulder.

Chapter Two

Cassidy screamed.

Before she could turn around, she glimpsed a gloved hand as the intruder slid an arm around her neck, yanked her back to his chest, placed a knife to her throat, slammed the front door. The blade bit skin, and the sting convinced Cassidy the man meant business. She held perfectly still, so frightened she could barely make her knees stiffen enough to hold her upright.

"There's two hundred dollars—"

"Silence."

The intruder put a black cap on Cassidy's head and pulled it down over her eyes, blinding her.

Oh, God. If he didn't want her money, what did he want? Cassidy knew the statistics. One in three women would be raped during their lifetime, but she'd never expected it to happen to her. In her own house. Without a chance to fight back.

Her brain kicked into overdrive. She shouldn't fight. The fact that he'd bothered to blindfold her was so she couldn't identify him. He probably intended to let her go.

Eventually.

She considered screaming again. But her neighbors wouldn't hear her through the thick plaster walls or over the lawn mower still roaring next door.

She was on her own.

Cassidy trembled, her mouth dry as sandpaper, her stomach full of bile. She told herself not to fight, but the moment the knife left her throat, her instinct for self-preservation took over. She was no martyr. She had to try to save herself.

She swung her hips and shoulder to one side. Simultaneously she stomped on his foot and got lucky, digging her heel into his toes.

The man cursed. But blocked the front door.

She had only seconds and lunged to the right as she lifted the cap from her eyes. Picking up a vase as she ran, she threw it over her shoulder and heard the pane of glass beside the front door shatter.

Sliding across the front hallway, she knocked a chair into his path, raced through the dining room and back through the kitchen. If she could just make it to the porch door.

A gun's chamber clicked. "Take another step and I'll shoot."

Cassidy dived toward the doorknob. She heard the hiss of a bullet, which lodged in the door in front of her. Cassidy skidded to a halt.

"Turn around and you're a dead woman."

Cassidy froze. She still hadn't seen the man's face, just a gloved hand. She didn't dare turn around as the footsteps approached. The cap came down over her head again, blinding her. The man gripped her arm, shoved her into a chair, tied her hands behind her back.

This couldn't be happening. She would wake up from the nightmare at any moment. Blind, helpless, Cassidy fought back, fear howling through her. "What do you want?"

"Who do you work for?"

The question arrowed another shot of terror through her. That familiar question wasn't what she'd expected, but she was too frightened to recall just where she'd heard it before. "I don't work for anyone."

The sudden slap of a palm against her face made her ears ring and her eyes tear. The man spoke as casually as if inviting her to breakfast. "We can do this the easy way or the hard way. It doesn't matter much to me."

Cassidy twisted her wrists in their bonds, but she couldn't even hope to get free. There was no slack in the ties. Her wrists were already going numb. "I'll tell you whatever you want to know. Please don't hurt me."

"Who do you work for?" the man asked again.

The man's tone was cold as death. She knew better than to give the same answer as she had before; that would only earn her another brutal slap.

"My father died last year. I inherited his law practice."

Another brutal slap on the other cheek slammed her head sideways. Cassidy tasted blood in her mouth.

"I don't care about your daddy. Who do you work for?"

"You mean my clients?"

Cassidy practiced family law. She didn't defend murderers or drug smugglers. She couldn't imagine which one of her clients this man was interested in. Could barely think with her head ringing, her cheeks on fire. But the sickening fear in her stomach was the worst.

Her tormentor's voice was too cold, too professional to give her any hope of getting out of this alive. At first she'd thought the blindfold was to prevent her from identifying him but now she suspected he just wanted her terrified so she'd talk. His tactics were working. She felt icy cold and burning hot at the same time.

She had the horrible feeling that as soon as she told him what he wanted to know, he'd put a bullet in her brain.

He could spend the entire day beating her.

She lived alone.

Didn't expect company.

And she had no idea what he wanted.

Again he asked the dreaded question. "Who do you work for?"

And again she had no answer.

AFTER PERUSING THE PAPERS Cassidy had dumped at his feet, Jake packed them up and heaved them into the trunk of his car, his anger slowly cooling. She'd offered to help him, and like it or not, he really needed that help, not just her legal expertise, but her common sense. Even if she had every right to be furious with him, he hoped after he apologized, she'd forgive him.

He made the thirty-minute drive from Half Moon

Bay to Crescent Cove in less than twenty minutes. While he knew Cassidy would probably rather see the abominable snowman than him showing up at her house uninvited, Jake owed her an apology. She'd done him a favor, and in return, he'd blamed her for her father's actions and implied that she was a liar. Inexcusable behavior under any circumstances. And he had no excuse. Except that she'd pushed all his buttons, reminding him of his failures, reminding him of one of the worst nights of his life.

That extraordinary summer he'd never even kissed Cassidy, but that hadn't stopped him from dreaming about sex and love the way most eighteen-year-old boys do. But unlike most boys who'd grown up with the love of family around them, Jake had never had anyone tell him that they'd loved him—not since he'd been five and his father had died. No one had ever told him he'd done a good job. No one had ruffled his hair with affection or hugged him. If anyone touched him at all, it had been a fist to the chin, an elbow to the gut.

So he'd craved affection. Maybe he'd read more into her emotions than had been there. He'd been so hungry for love that when she'd called him that long-ago afternoon to tell him she had special news and a special evening planned, he'd hoped and dreamed that they might make love.

He'd bought a few candles to hide the dingy walls of his room, changed the sheets and spent his last few dollars to borrow a radio from another boarder. Freshly showered after a ten-hour day slinging hamburgers, he'd met Cassidy at his door. She'd taken his hand and dragged him down to the park where they could watch the stars in the balmy Floridian moonlight.

After blowing out the candles, he'd followed willingly enough. She'd brought a blanket and a picnic dinner, but he'd been too excited to fill his ever-hungry stomach. He'd hoped she wanted a little romance before they went back to his room. He could still recall her aroma, wildflowers and honey, her lips scented of strawberry lipstick. But most of all he'd craved her golden heat. Cassidy's skin was always warm to his touch, and he could never seem to resist holding her hand or running his fingers through her silky hair. Under a crescent moon he'd leaned over to kiss her, as ready as a volcano to burst with wanting her. And she'd pulled away.

When he'd suggested going back to his room, she'd turned over and told him she was heading to UCLA in California in two weeks. And his world crashed. Hard. Without Cassidy to brighten his dreary nights, the two jobs he worked each week to make ends meet seemed unbearable. California might as well have been Mars. Four years and three thousand miles would effectively separate them and end their relationship just as her father had intended, since Jake couldn't afford to follow her to California. Even after he joined Special Forces, he hadn't been able to put her out of his mind.

Cassidy had been the first person to show him affection or friendship for thirteen years, and losing her had devastated him. He'd coped with the emptiness by working harder. In what little spare time he had after his honorable discharge from the military, Jake had searched for his sisters and developed the skills to open his own detective agency. But no matter how many hours he'd worked, he'd never forgotten that bright summer when anything and everything had seemed possible. And he'd never forgotten what it felt like to wake up in the morning and look forward to Cassidy's smile brightening his day.

Jake drove up to Cassidy's house and saw a broken windowpane next to the front door. His instinct for trouble immediately kicked in. Maybe a kid had thrown a baseball through the pane. But why was the glass still glinting on the front stoop?

There could be a dozen reasons. The likeliest was that Cassidy wasn't home.

Still, Jake had learned to take precautions. He drove past the house and parked down the street. Picking up his cell phone, he called his friend and number-one employee, Harrison Gordon, and quickly gave him his location.

"If you don't hear from me within four minutes, send the cops."

Ever cautious, the former police office from Dade County asked, "Want backup?"

"Cassidy may be in trouble. Phone's in my pocket. I'll leave the line open."

"Be careful."

Jake clipped the phone to his belt, eased his gun from his ankle holster and slipped it into his pocket. He didn't want to chance scaring Cassidy if it wasn't necessary. And a bullet could shoot through fabric as easily as air.

Moving quickly and silently, Jake approached the ranch-style house from the side, slipping easily behind the shrubbery and ducking beneath the windows.

Normally he would have scouted the perimeter and waited for backup, but he had a bad feeling in his gut.

When he approached the broken glass by the front door, he heard the sickening sound of a slap against flesh and a woman's yelp of pain.

Sweat popped out on his brow. Every cell in his body yearned to burst through the door. But he wouldn't do Cassidy an ounce of good if he got himself or her shot before he could rescue her.

Jake took a moment to reach for his phone. "I'm going in, Harrison. Get me backup. Fast."

"Wait—"

Jake didn't listen to the rest of Harrison's warning. He eased through the door, gun first. Glass crunched under his shoes. Jake silently swore. He'd just given up the element of surprise.

At least the sickening sounds of the assault had stopped. But Jake couldn't wait for the cops to arrive. It only took a nanosecond to end a life. Cassidy's future might hinge on his next decision. Jake didn't hesitate. He just wished he knew how many opponents he was up against and if they were armed.

Ducking through a doorway, Jake stepped lightly into the dining room. He quickly scanned the thick draperies. Saw no sign of feet peeking out beneath the bottom.

Keeping low, he dodged down a hallway and rolled into the kitchen. A bullet hissed past his ear. But he had heard no gunshot. Obviously the intruder used a silencer—unusual for a street thug.

Out of the corner of his eye, Jake glimpsed Cassidy blindfolded by a cap, tied to a kitchen chair. Her shoulders slumped. He had no way of knowing if she was still breathing, and his heart missed a beat.

Think. Cassidy needed him to be professional.

Estimating that the gunfire had come from the direction of the refrigerator, Jake scrambled to the position least likely to put Cassidy in the line of fire.

In the distance, police sirens sounded. Two more bullets kept Jake behind the counter. He heard footsteps retreating. The back door squeaked open and then more footsteps pounded across the patio, indicating the intruder had run away.

Normally Jake would have pursued the culprit. But no way could he leave Cassidy blindfolded and tied to that chair, wondering if she was going to live or die. Not even for another minute.

Jake hurried to her and yanked the cap from her head. "Sunshine, talk to me. Are you all right?"

Dazed blue eyes looked at him with fear. Blood trickled from her mouth. "Jake?"

She was alive! Pleasure shot through him, but as much as he yearned to gather her into his arms, touch that golden skin, inhale her feminine scent and reassure himself that she was all right, he hesitated. He had no desire to renew the old feelings, sensations and emotions that touching her had once caused.

"Someone hit me."

"He won't anymore. Not ever again. I'm here now, Sunshine."

He ached to pull her into his arms and hold her tenderly, but he shoved aside his needs, his urge to comfort her by touch and satisfy himself she was unharmed. Instead, he knelt and untied her hands and used his voice to give reassurance. "You're safe.

Whoever hit you went out the back door. I assume there was just one?''

Cassidy rubbed her wrists slowly but didn't attempt to rise from the chair, reminding him of a wild bird caged too long and afraid to fly free. Banishing his own fears at what touching her might do to his turbulent emotions, Jake reached for her, but she twisted away, terror darkening her eyes and arrowing straight to his core.

Jake ignored her automatic rejection and how much his insides churned. She needed time to recover, time to collect herself. While she watched him with suspicion, he gave up trying to touch her again.

Jake took his phone off the belt clip. ''Harrison, you still there?''

''Yes, boss.''

''Inform the cops that the suspect fled the area on foot. We're okay in here.''

Distrust still clouding her eyes, Cassidy looked from the gun in Jake's hand to the phone in the other. Her voice came out like a croak. ''What are you doing here?''

''Explanations can wait. An ambulance is on the way. But let me see to that cut on your lip.'' Jake took a clean dish towel, ran water over it, rinsed it out, then wrapped ice in it. He handed it to her. ''Place this where it hurts.''

''Everything hurts.'' Eyes narrowed, Cassidy stared at his gun as if she feared he'd shoot her any second.

Jake put on the safety, then handed her his weapon, butt first. ''Smell my gun. It hasn't been fired. Someone else attacked you, Sunshine. I would never hurt you.''

She sniffed the gun, and just the fact that she couldn't take his word squeezed Jake's emotions all over again. But he felt better when some of the fear left her eyes. He also realized how innocent she was. If he *had* been the intruder, he could have had two weapons.

Cassidy didn't seem to have the strength to hold the ice to her swollen lip. Slowly he knelt beside her. "Here, let me do that."

This time she allowed him to touch her. Jake gently eased the ice pack from her lip to her cheeks where bruises were already darkening beneath her golden skin. What kind of bastard struck a helpless woman across the face?

His expression must have shown his anger, because Cassidy, eyes bleak, jerked away from him.

"You're going to be okay," he murmured. "We're going to install an alarm system in your house so this can never happen again. And one at your office, too."

"He was going to kill me," Cassidy muttered.

Jake wanted to question her, but recognized her dilated pupils as a sign of shock. He suspected that she barely knew what she was saying. So he just let her talk.

"He kept asking me who I worked for." Cassidy started to shake. "I'm so cold."

Jake swept her up into his arms and carried her into the den, her scent enveloping him, just as he'd feared, in old hungers, old needs. Ruthlessly he tried to ignore the softness of her breasts crushed against his chest, the silk of her hair against his neck.

Cassidy needed him, and he could no more ignore her pain than he could ignore a crying baby back in the orphanage. He sat on the sofa and wrapped an afghan around her. Cradling her head on his chest, he tried to warm her with his body heat, and the entire time he wondered how many sleepless nights this would cost him. Still, he'd gladly pay the price of turning and tossing for a year, if that was what it took to give her back her sense of safety.

"No more." She shivered, and when he kept the ice pressed to her face, she pushed it away.

"Ice will keep the swelling down. You don't want to mar that perfect complexion. Just bear the cold a little longer. You're strong. You can do that, Sunshine. Just a little longer, okay?"

He spoke soothingly, but she never relaxed, and her trembling frightened him. Maybe he shouldn't have moved her. She might be injured more badly than he'd thought.

Where the hell was that ambulance?

THE COPS SHOWED UP entirely too soon for Cassidy. She would have been content just to stay on Jake's lap, rest her head against his chest and let the security of his strong arms banish the horror of her ordeal.

Never before had she suffered pain that intense. Never before had she suffered such fear. Never before had she faced her mortality on such intimate terms.

She'd thought she was going to die, not in some indeterminable time in the future, but today. Although she'd never resigned herself to dying, she'd had no hope. She hadn't thought just of the past, of opportunities lost and old regrets, but of all the things she'd never experience. She'd hoped to fall in love. Have children. Grandchildren. And her future could have been taken from her, and she had no idea why.

Then, somehow, Jake had rescued her, and now she wanted to enjoy each priceless moment. Each breath seemed a gift, each caress of his fingers through her hair precious. And the future was once again filled with wondrous possibilities.

"Thank you for saving my life."

"I was happy to do it, Sunshine. I just wish I'd caught the bastard."

Thanking Jake wasn't enough. He'd given her the invaluable gift of time, and she wanted him to understand. She could hear the police coming down her street, but she wanted Jake to know how she felt before they arrived.

"Have you ever been sick?"

"Not often," Jake admitted, "but a few times."

Pleased that he didn't seem disturbed by her strange choice of topic, she continued, "Remember all the things you missed? How food didn't taste good? How you didn't feel up to a walk on the beach or making a momentous decision?" She tilted her head back and gazed into his warm amber eyes. "Remember how good it felt to get well again? To move with energy and determination, to laugh?"

As if he couldn't forget what had almost happened to her, Jake looked down at her without smiling. "The newness and wonder of feeling healthy again never lasts. We soon forget and go on as before."

"Exactly."

Jake had always been quick to catch on to the threads of her thoughts and weave them together into meaningful ideas.

"I don't ever want to forget how precious life is," she said. "I don't want to waste another minute."

Jake cocked an arrogant eyebrow and his sexy mouth curved upward in amusement. "You always did live for today, Sunshine."

"There have been lost opportunities."

"Is that so?" he murmured, his voice purring like a cat in her ear.

"Things I did and things I didn't."

"Like what?"

"I've always wanted to travel and I never had the time."

"Where do you want to go?"

"Tahiti, Europe, the Far East."

"What else?"

"I want children. I want to leave this world knowing I changed it somehow."

"You still have time for kids."

"Thanks to you." But she'd never found the right time and the right man to have those kids with. She hesitated to say more, but then decided to tell him the rest. She wasn't sure why she wanted to tell him, but after almost dying, the world seemed bright and clean, and she wanted to start over with a fresh slate. And maybe, just maybe, she was testing him, to see his reaction.

"And I regret that we didn't keep in touch. I've missed you." She said the words in an impulsive burst of emotion before she could change her mind. As Jake's tender expression turned to stone, his eyes shadowed with thoughts she couldn't read, she shrugged away the hurt she felt when he didn't say, *I missed you, too.*

Knowing Jake had trouble voicing sentimental feelings, she made peace with his silence, placed her cheek against his chest, took comfort in the strong beat of his heart. But she couldn't regret her boldness. She felt a rapport with Jake that hadn't diminished over time. Telling Jake her thoughts and feelings had always been easy. That she'd returned to Florida without bothering to renew their friendship had been a mistake. A mistake she intended to rectify if Jake would let her. She was no longer an innocent eighteen-year-old who needed to follow her childhood dream, but a grown woman who'd achieved her goals and could now make her own choices.

Yet, with her outspoken revelation, the closeness between them ended. The air of intimacy vanished.

Jake had withdrawn from her. He might still be holding her on his lap, but his fingers no longer combed through her hair. He no longer curled his arms protectively around her. A stillness surrounded him, practically encasing him in ice.

But it was the emotional distance that had grown as vast as the Gulf of Mexico. Jake had a way of closing off the world, closing off his emotions, from others, from her, maybe even from himself.

"This is Officer Silvero. Everyone okay in there?" a man called out.

Jake's gestures were gentle, yet more efficient than tender, as he lifted her off his lap and placed her beside him on the sofa. Then, back straight, shoulders squared, he stood to greet the cop. "We're in the den and all right."

By the time the police officer entered the room, Jake had his detective identification out of his pocket.

Cassidy watched him shake hands with a young earnest-looking officer who couldn't be much older than twenty, and she heard Jake murmur, "Go easy on her." Then Jake leaned forward and whispered something she couldn't hear in the cop's ear.

"I may be in shock, but I can answer your questions, Officer," Cassidy said. She knew Jake was probably trying to protect her, but she preferred knowing the facts, no matter how bad a picture those facts painted. She'd never believed in hiding from the truth or letting others take on her problems, and was slightly annoyed with Jake for attempting to do so, even if she did understand his motives.

"I'm Silvero. My partner, Jonesy, is looking around out back. Would you prefer to speak with a female officer, ma'am?"

Cassidy shook her head and regretted it as her skull throbbed. "I wasn't raped. But I won't be able to help much, since I can't identify the man who..."

She stopped and realized this was going to be harder to retell than she'd anticipated. As she'd spoken, images rose to haunt her. Helplessness at being tied. Fear that she had no idea what the man wanted from her. Horror that she would most likely die after a short period of intense suffering. The telling would make her relive the incident—one she badly wanted to forget.

Always sensitive, Jake seemed to understand her difficulty. He leaned close, but didn't touch her. Instead, he used the soothing tone that had calmed her before. "There's no rush, Sunshine. You can wait until tomorrow."

Silvero took out a pad of paper. "Now would be

better, sir. She may forget something important by tomorrow.''

"I won't forget," Cassidy said, and then looked at Jake, who clearly stood ready to protect her. "And I'd like to get this over with."

But the ambulance had finally arrived. Cassidy insisted she didn't need to go to the hospital, and after checking her pulse and her pupils, the medic agreed. "Don't drink any alcohol for twenty-four hours. If you feel dizzy, have someone take you to the hospital or call 911.

After the medics left, Cassidy quickly told the officer her story, but this time she was detached, pushing her emotions aside. A trick she'd learned when she'd been in law school and had dealt with some unpleasant cases.

She summed up the horrifying incident by sticking to the facts and squashing her emotions in the back of her mind. The effort sapped her energy, and she'd never felt so tired, as though all her muscles had gone to sleep, but she continued through to the end.

"You never saw the intruder?" Silvero asked again when she'd finished.

Cassidy knew better than to shake her head, since every time she did, the pain flared. "Either I was running and my back was to him, or my eyes were covered by the hat."

"You're positive it was a man?"

"Yes. He had a guttural voice. And he sounded educated."

The cop stopped writing and looked up. "What makes you say that?"

Cassidy paused, trying to remember. "His grammar was good."

Silvero started writing again. "Did he have an accent?"

"No."

The cop frowned and looked from Cassidy to Jake. "You sure it wasn't him that hit you?"

"Jake would never strike a woman," Cassidy said.

Jake sighed as if he'd expected the question. "I'm carrying a weapon in my ankle holster. I never fired it and I gave it to Cassidy to reassure her. Would you like to inspect my weapon, Officer?"

Silvero nodded. "Move slowly, sir."

Jake bent and handed the cop the weapon just as he'd done Cassidy. Suddenly she felt ashamed that the cop had questioned his honor. He'd saved her life. He didn't deserve to be questioned. "Jake's voice is different, deeper, than that of the man who hit me."

Jake gave him harder evidence than she could supply. "Once you dig the slugs from her wall, you'll see they don't match my gun."

The officer took Jake's weapon and sniffed. Finally he handed it back to Jake. "How did you happen to come along when you did?"

"I needed to finish an earlier discussion between Cassidy and me."

Their earlier discussion had been over! Jake had practically thrown her out of his house. Why had he come to her home uninvited, showing up at exactly the right time? Cassidy had seen movies where one man did the dirty work and the other befriended a mark to set up a sting. Although Jake had been furious with her earlier, he had no reason to do that to her.

Jake had once told her how the orphanage unfairly punished children. How he'd often taken onto his shoulders blame that wasn't his. He couldn't have changed that much. Besides, after the way he'd gently tended to her, she knew he'd never ever condone violence. Although Jake could be evasive, he was never sneaky or underhanded.

Jake answered the cop, speaking stiffly, shoulders thrown back and defiant. Cassidy sensed how much he disliked this inquisition and how useless he felt it to be. But he remained polite, if aloof.

Cassidy lost track of the interrogation and was jerked back to the present when the cop cleared his throat. "Ma'am?"

"I'm sorry. What was the question?"

"Can you think of anyone who could have done this to you? An ex-husband or former lover? A client?"

"I'm a small-town lawyer. Mostly I draw up wills and trusts, handle real-estate transactions, that sort of thing. I've never done criminal work or been married. And my last relationship ended amicably several years ago."

Cassidy had mixed feelings about the cops going through her home, and once again she was glad Jake was with her. While she appreciated the extra police protection, it seemed an invasion of her privacy to have strangers roaming through her home and asking about her private life. She wanted to close this episode and put it behind her.

Jake folded his arms over his chest and spoke to

Officer Silvero. "Enough. She's tired. Let her rest, and if she thinks of anything else, she'll call. You have a business card?"

The officer reluctantly closed his notepad. Cassidy sensed that if not for Jake's intervention, the cop would have questioned her all day.

The officer handed her his card and looked around. "Don't touch the slugs. I'll have the crime team dig them out later. No point dusting for prints since the man wore gloves, right?" Cassidy nodded and he continued, "Perhaps you could call a friend over to spend the night?"

Jake shook his head. "She won't be staying here."

Cassidy almost objected aloud to his high-handed tactics, then decided to remain quiet. She'd rather discuss her living arrangements with Jake after the cop left. Maybe by then she'd recover some strength. Besides, she wasn't eager to stay here alone. Not unless the police caught the intruder, and that seemed less likely by the minute.

After Officer Silvero and his partner left, Jake straddled a chair across from her. "I'm going to have a security system installed tomorrow. Until then, you can stay with me."

"The security system sounds fine, and I appreciate your offer." Cassidy hesitated, then blurted, "Jake, there's something I didn't tell the police."

Chapter Three

"You forgot to tell the cops that you're into kinky sex?" Jake's teasing comment came out of nowhere. He was just hoping to ease her tension.

She humored him with a smile that didn't reach her eyes. "Nothing so scandalous."

"You made an illegal U-turn on the way home?"

He didn't like the paleness of her skin beneath the tan and wanted to see the glow come back. Even more, he wanted to return their friendship to an even keel and forget her words about how she'd wished they'd kept in touch. At night for months after she'd gone off to college, he'd thought of little more than what it would have been like to touch her and have her touch him in return.

He didn't want those fantasies in his head. Besides, Cassidy had been frightened. Hurt. In shock. And while he didn't believe that her remarks reflected anything beyond a desire for a platonic friendship, he suspected that her words would haunt his dreams for weeks.

"Jake, stop teasing me." She rested her head back

on the sofa and her golden hair spilled over her shoulders. "When I left your place, I was angry with you."

"That's why I came here. To apologize for my bad behavior. Even if your father refused to talk to me, I had no right to blame you for his actions. To practically call you a liar was going way too far. I'm sorry."

"Apology accepted. I'd say you've more than made up for your rudeness by saving my life." Cassidy shuddered, then raised her chin, and her eyes darkened with determination. "I thought I'd dumped the box's entire contents at your feet—"

He chuckled. "A highly dramatic gesture that helped me come to my senses."

"—but one of the papers stayed in the box. A paper with a phone number."

"You called that number?" he guessed, neither the least bit surprised by her impulsiveness nor bothered that she hadn't returned to give it to him—not in the dark mood he'd been in. But he'd set those old painful memories aside. He'd moved on with his life. And part of moving on meant realizing that Cassidy had never felt about him the way he'd once felt about her. She'd considered him a friend and had never wanted more. He'd been the one who'd once wanted more, but he hadn't been willing to show her how he'd really felt and risk losing her friendship. But that was all a long time ago.

He was different now, not so afraid to risk what he had to get what he wanted. But had Cassidy changed? Was she still the same person he remembered? Did she see him as the friend he'd once been? Or did she see him as a man with wants and needs and desires?

Cassidy's sweet voice drew him from his thoughts. "The woman who answered my call asked for a password. I had no idea what she was talking about, so I just read the words off the slip of paper."

A password? He shoved aside thoughts about the past and concentrated on the present. Cassidy had his full attention. "What password?"

"I can't remember. The paper's in my purse in the kitchen, I think."

Jake retrieved her purse and watched her dig through it. She was starting to recover from her ordeal. Slowly her voice was regaining some strength, her shoulders were slumping less. And he could only admire her courage.

Cassidy had grown up in a secure home with loving parents who'd given her every advantage in life. Yet she wasn't spoiled. She'd had to live with setbacks and a few hard knocks. After her mother's death from cancer, she'd shown a resilience that was a testament to Frazier Atkins's fathering skills. And if the man had become overprotective of his daughter, Jake wouldn't have blamed him—except that overprotectiveness had sliced Cassidy from Jake's life.

While Cassidy might be facing her own mortality for the first time, she wasn't just coping. She was thinking with all eight cylinders. And just like ten years ago, her primary thoughts weren't revolving around him.

At least she seemed willing and able to keep her thoughts trained on business. Right now, Jake couldn't afford the distraction of brooding over the past, not when Cassidy's life might be at stake.

"Here it is!" She handed him the paper. "'Blow

back.' That's what I said, and the woman connected me. There was a long wait. Finally a man answered and asked who I worked for.'' Cassidy's eyes suddenly grew wide, her words rushed out with a burst of excitement. "That's what I couldn't remember. The man who broke in asked the same exact question as the person at this number. Both wanted to know who I worked for.''

But Cassidy didn't work for anybody. What the hell was going on?

It could have been a coincidence, but Jake didn't believe it. He'd spent too long as a detective, too long investigating the seamier side of life on behalf of his clients not to recognize a tenuous connection. Something in that box, someone Cassidy had called, had placed her life in danger.

She'd almost died because she'd done him a favor. ''If you hadn't tried to help me, you wouldn't be in danger.''

She warily looked at the windows, then squared her shoulders. ''The intruder is gone. Who says I'm still in danger?''

''I think your phone call triggered the intruder's showing up on your doorstep, but he didn't get what he wanted.''

Cassidy's forehead wrinkled in a frown. ''But I don't work for anyone. I didn't know what he wanted.''

''But if *he* thinks you have the answers he wants, he may come back.'' Jake dragged a hand through his hair, weighing possibilities and options.

''Maybe we need to tell the police,'' Cassidy suggested.

"We have nothing solid. Even if they believed us, the Crescent Cove police department doesn't have the manpower to pursue an investigation." Jake scowled at the thought of law enforcement, of policemen grilling Cassidy and himself about his past, asking questions they couldn't answer. Jake dialed his cell phone, the paper Cassidy had given him still in his hand. "Harrison, you still have that friend at the phone company?"

Harrison groaned. "It'll cost me a dinner and dancing."

"You can use the exercise," Jake quipped. "I want you to trace this call." Jake gave Harrison the number. "I'll pay for the dinner."

"But how're you going to pay for my aching feet?"

After Jake hung up, Cassidy looked up at him, her eyes thoughtful. "I think we should go through the box's contents carefully. Maybe there will be clues that can tell us what's going on. I know you didn't want my help, I know you blame my father for not giving you the box ten years ago, but we have to go on. My life may be at stake. I feel as if I'm entitled to see this through. Don't make me wait alone while you search for answers. Please, Jake?"

He could ignore neither her fear nor her sincerity. And still he hesitated. "You might be in more danger if you help me."

She countered with direct simplicity. "I feel safer with you than without you."

Her words brought back that warm glow in his gut, but he suspected she would have said the same to any man who'd saved her. She wasn't speaking on a personal level of emotion, but out of concern for her physical safety. "You aren't a qualified detective, Sunshine."

"I won't get in your way."

Negotiations began. And she'd sidestepped the issue of her lack of qualifications. A lawyer tactic. But they weren't in court. They were out in the real world, a world where the players often had their own set of rules. Rules she wouldn't fathom. Rules that could get them killed.

While he sensed her determination, he could be just as determined. While he'd offered to let her stay with him for one night, he didn't want her underfoot, a constant reminder of the hurt she'd caused him in the past, during an investigation that could take days or weeks. "But you won't take orders, either, Sunshine. You always do what you think is best."

"Doesn't everyone?" She didn't bother to deny his words, and his admiration for her rose another notch.

Jake shook his head, glanced out the window at the palms swaying in the breeze, then back at her. "A client would let me lead the way, since I do have over ten years of experience."

She fingered the snap on her purse. Her fingers shook slightly and then she balled them into a fist. "You aren't going to leave me alone. I'm scared like I've never been before. That maniac might come back. And this time I might not be lucky enough to be rescued. I don't want to spend the rest of my life looking over my shoulder. I want to help you find that man and put him in jail where he belongs."

She cradled her trembling fist in her other hand, trying to prevent it from shaking, and his heart went out to her. First her mother had died, then her father, leaving her alone in the world. Better than anyone, Jake could empathize with Cassidy. He knew what it was like to be alone, without family. He responded to the fear in her voice by offering another solution, one that would keep her safe, yet at a distance from him. "We could hire a bodyguard. Get you round-the-clock protection."

Cassidy stood and faced him, her hands on her hips. "That's not good enough. I don't want to live like that. So here's the deal, Jake. Either you let me help you, or..."

"Or what?"

"I'll hire another private investigator and follow the clues on my own."

He had no doubt she would do just as she promised. Still, he tested her resolve, made his voice deliberately harsh. "I don't respond to ultimatums."

"And I don't respond to death threats." Her eyes flashed with anger. "Do we have a deal?"

"MAYBE WE'LL BOTH think better on a full stomach. How about dinner?" Jake asked, his tone polite, his manner reserved.

As he drove her to a local bar and grill, Cassidy tried to think of ways to convince him to let her tag along while he searched for his sisters and for clues as to why she'd been attacked. She knew he'd respond to her fear more than her arguments. Jake had a soft spot for the underdog that she'd exploited with a mercilessness that surprised her. She'd taken advantage of her knowledge of Jake's past, deliberately allowing her fear to show. Jake had once told her that in the orphanage, he'd helped comfort those kids who needed it, protected them from bullies, always hoping that someone else was protecting his sisters as he protected those close to him. In her fear, she'd shamelessly exploited Jake's vulnerability, but Cassidy didn't regret her actions. She hadn't faked her fear. She could hide her terror if necessary, but she wouldn't rest easy until the man who'd attacked her was behind bars.

On the way to dinner, she countered Jake's every argument. She told him she could put her law practice on hold and take several weeks off. She hated to leave her pro bono work at the women's clinic, but they'd have to manage without her. If she stayed with Jake, her routine would be less predictable.

Entering the restaurant, a place where locals hung out and tourists rarely found, they delayed their discussion while Jimmy Buffet's music serenaded them with promises of Margaritaville. A waitress seated them next to a window overlooking the parking lot and a two-lane road that wound along the coast. She told them that due to the drought, water was available only upon request. Cassidy took a seat and consulted the menu. She ordered shrimp and—wishing for a glass of wine, but recalling the medic's instructions not to drink alcohol—a club soda with a lime wedge.

The hot food came promptly. The view might not be great, but the atmosphere and fresh seafood were wonderful.

Cassidy finished off her last spicy shrimp. "Before you came over to my house, did you look through the stuff I brought?"

Jake washed his blackened-grouper sandwich down

with sweet tea, then pushed back from the table. "I haven't read the three diaries my mother left yet. There are several photographs that don't mean anything to me, but the copies of my sisters' birth certificates and my parents' marriage license will provide my chief investigator with a good place to start looking for information."

Just as Cassidy finished her coffee, Jake's cell phone rang. He checked the caller identification, then answered. "What have you got, Harrison?"

Cassidy couldn't hear the other man's reply, but Jake's face lit up. "You do? That's terrific. Hold on." Jake whipped a pen from his pocket and furiously wrote names and addresses on a napkin. "Has the lady at the telephone company come through? Okay, keep working on it."

Jake hung up, his face flushed with success, the color high on his sharp cheekbones. "After you left my house, I faxed Harrison copies of my sisters' birth certificates. He's traced the adoption records."

"But they're sealed."

"Harrison knows people everywhere. It's his job to dig out information not readily accessible."

"So tell me," she prodded, not in the least surprised by his assistant's ingenuity. She was sure that Jake ran a sharp operation. That he'd become so successful after starting from nothing made her feel a great deal of pride. And Jake had a gift for friendship. Look how easily she'd accepted his help, just as the orphans had so long ago.

Jake was a natural leader, but he also held himself apart. Sharing had always been difficult for him.

"I have my sisters' current addresses." Jake's

voice was infused with happiness and excitement and wonder. "I never expected my search to end so soon."

"Are you going to call them?" Cassidy asked, enjoying his pleasure and the sparkle of amber light in his eyes, emitting a warmth that wrapped her like a soft blanket. Jake's sharing anything with her after all these years and showing her his pleasure were a gift. A gift of part of himself.

Jake sighed and threaded a hand through his hair. "I think a letter would be best."

Such extraordinary patience. That he would be willing to wait to introduce himself to his sisters surprised her. "Why write when you can call?"

"News that my sisters have siblings may come as a shock. A letter will let them adjust gradually to the idea before speaking with me."

He sounded as if he'd thought through every potentiality. For Jake's sake, she hoped his sisters responded positively and soon. In his place, she didn't know if she would be so patient or thoughtful or understanding.

"I'll leave it up to them if and when to contact me."

He'd waited so long. She couldn't believe he didn't intend to pick up the phone and just call, even if only to hear their voices. Jake also had extraordinary composure. In his place, she would have dialed, too excited to consider the consequences. While Jake had never forgotten his boyhood promise to his father, hadn't given up his search all these years, he was methodical, careful. But she just couldn't comprehend how he could bear to wait until they contacted him now that he'd found them. However, Cassidy realized this decision had to be his. She had no right to try to change his mind.

Jake's eyes narrowed, and he suddenly stood and tossed money on the table. "Let's go."

Alarmed by his sudden reversal of tone and demeanor, Cassidy looked past Jake toward the parking lot. Her stomach tightened.

Two men had just pulled up in a four-door sedan. She watched them exit the vehicle. Each man sported a suit and tie.

Jake grabbed Cassidy's hand. "The bulges beneath their armpits indicate they're carrying."

"Carrying?"

"Guns."

Jake shouldered his way past customers eating with enjoyment, waitresses carrying plates of lobster tails, crab claws and grouper sandwiches, and headed for the rear of the restaurant. Without hesitation she followed, allowing him to pull her into the kitchen.

They hurried past gleaming stainless-steel countertops, a stove with a huge cauldron of soup and a kid sweeping the floor. Jake swiped a bottle of wine off a wire rack and tossed the chef a twenty-dollar bill. The surprised cook shook his head at their crazy antics.

Fear lodged in her throat, Cassidy hurried to keep up with Jake's long strides. She took a moment to look over her shoulder for their pursuers and slammed into Jake's broad back. "Sorry."

He'd halted to open the back door. "Hurry."

She scooted through the door, realizing now was not the time to ask questions. But Jake had parked his vehicle out front. They'd have to go around the building to reach it, and they'd likely be seen by the men in suits. Cassidy wondered if they were FBI, the mob, hired guns or if one of them was the same man who had tied her to her kitchen chair. She didn't want to stick around long enough to find out.

She slipped behind the restaurant, next to a Dumpster, and the scent of rotting fish slapped her in the face. The empty lot behind the restaurant provided extra parking for weekend overflow, but she saw no place to hide. Before she could turn and ask Jake where to head next, he'd whacked the neck off the wine bottle, stuffed a handkerchief into the now-open neck and down into the red wine, then urged her around the corner.

"Be ready to run to my car on my signal." He spoke as calmly as he'd previously ordered their dinner.

How could he remain so calm when her pulse was beating so hard that she had trouble hearing him? Breathless, she inhaled deeply and frowned. "What signal?"

"I'll tell you. Just be ready."

When the men in suits reached the back door, Jake lit the handkerchief with a lighter and tossed it toward the Dumpster.

"Now! Go."

Cassidy raced along the side of the restaurant toward the parking lot and Jake's car.

Behind her, the bottle shattered. Wine must have spilled everywhere, spreading flames inside the Dumpster. The noise, louder than she'd expected, urged her feet faster while a smoky haze wafted on a stiff breeze and spread over the lot. She worried that fear would root her feet to the pavement, but adrenaline thrust her watery knees onward.

Jake's diversion would buy them only seconds. But all they needed were seconds to reach his car. His remote starter had already warmed up the engine by the time she slid into the passenger seat and locked her door.

Before she could fasten her seat belt, Jake joined her, and they peeled out of the parking lot, heading north. Stomach lurching, she looked over her shoulder and cringed. The men were already in their sedan and right behind them.

"Don't worry, this Mercedes will outrun them."

The speed of his car was the least of their problems, she thought.

"Just watch out for the snowbirds," she reminded him. The retired folks who flocked to Florida to avoid the harsh winters in the northern U.S. and Canada tended to drive slowly. Traffic often crawled along the highway at twenty miles an hour. Jake's speedometer was hitting sixty.

"Who are those guys?" Cassidy asked as she peered back at the silver sedan.

"I have no idea. Can you see the driver?"

"They're too far back," Cassidy told him.

Jake passed a water truck, a motorcyclist and another car before hanging a right.

"Where're you going?"

"They might have another vehicle up ahead ready to cut us off. I thought I'd take the bridge."

The barrier islands along the coast of St. Petersburg were connected to the mainland by a series of bridges over the intracoastal waterway. Tourists skated and fished along the sidewalks, and vendors hawked ice cream. If they could make it off the island and onto a major highway without being intercepted, they stood a good chance of eluding their pursuers.

Cassidy prayed the bridge wouldn't be held open for a sailboat to pass under and back up the traffic for half a mile. Gritting her teeth as Jake passed another car, she finally snapped her seat belt into place. But she didn't feel any more secure.

"Maybe we should just drive to the police station."

"Then they'd know where we were, and they could wait until we left, and we'd be sitting ducks."

"Why do you have so little confidence in the police?"

Jake swerved around a truck. "They're undertrained, understaffed and underpaid. That's why I'm in business."

"Jake?"

"Yes?"

She swallowed hard and shut her eyes as he steered to avoid a cyclist. Bravely she opened her eyes and looked at Jake. "Do you think the same man who attacked me is following us?"

"Maybe." Jake cocked his head to the side as he considered her suggestion. Hands relaxed on the wheel, he could have been out for a Sunday drive. By just looking at him, she never would have guessed they were being pursued. Jake drove up to the tollbooth and tossed change into the basket. "I wish Harrison could trace that phone number you found so we'd have an idea who we're dealing with."

"They're organized. That man showed up at my

house less than half an hour after I made the phone call.'' Cassidy swayed to the left and pointed to a woman pushing a baby carriage along the bridge. ''Watch out!''

Jake veered, then sped over the bridge to the other side just before a three-deck yacht honked its horn to signal the bridge master it needed passage and an opened bridge. Behind them, blinking red lights on bars came down across the road, stopping traffic and the silver sedan. The bridge started to open and traffic had to wait, allowing Jake and Cassidy at least a fifteen-minute advantage.

She breathed a sigh of relief as Jake slowed their speed to normal and merged with the regular flow of traffic. ''Now what?''

''I want to find a print shop.''

She glanced at Jake, wondering what he was up to. He seemed unperturbed by their close call or by the ease with which those men had found them at the restaurant. He'd come a long way from the boy she'd once known. She wondered how many dangers he'd faced and how they had shaped him into the man who sat beside her so calmly and competently, the man who displayed no fear. His steady hands kept them moving forward. In the dusky reddish-orange of the setting sun, his face looked darker, his chiseled cheekbones honed from granite. She knew that look. Jake was thinking about his sisters.

To be safe, Jake made several turns over the next thirty minutes, exited a freeway and reversed his course before taking the ramp and heading into one of those twenty-four-hour print shops. Opening the trunk, he took out a briefcase stuffed with the items she'd brought him this morning.

Had it been only this morning? It seemed like days. And Jake had slipped back into her life as easily as he had once before. She didn't mind his silences or even his brooding. She didn't mind the way she often had to pull answers from him. And she didn't mind that he shared his thoughts so reluctantly, because it made them all the more precious when he did.

But the man at her side was different in several respects from the boy she'd known. He no longer had the spontaneity he'd once had. Instead, he chose his words carefully, weighed his actions with an intensity that made her wonder if he'd suffered some tragedy during the intervening years.

Jake held open the door for her to the beckoning bright lights of the print shop. "I want to copy everything you brought me and send it to my sisters with a letter."

Cassidy stepped inside the print shop. "But you haven't had time to go through the material thoroughly."

"I know. But if anything did happen to us—not that I believe it will—I'd want my sisters to know about each other."

She understood his reasoning and didn't question him further. "I'll be happy to talk to the clerk about the copying while you write your letters," she volunteered, knowing he'd want to word his letter carefully. Or had he already planned what he wanted to say? She wouldn't be surprised if he'd already written the letter in his head, just so he would be set for this moment. Jake was that methodical and thorough. Perfect characteristics for a detective.

While Jake bought stationery and took up residence at a desk to write his letters, Cassidy made copies of the diaries on the self-service machines. It was slow-going. Although she could copy two pages at once by laying the diary facedown on the copier, she had to turn the pages by hand. Thirty minutes later Jake still hadn't finished his letters, so she asked a clerk to copy the photographs on a specialized machine in the back. The clerk, a student studying for a calculus test, put down his notebook to wait on her. When the clerk returned, he'd done such a good job that, except for the heavier paper on the originals, Cassidy couldn't tell the old ones from the duplicates.

Jake was done. He helped her pick out mailing supplies, added his letter to each sister's package and then carefully addressed them. Jake finished paying with his credit card just in time for the printer's evening parcel pickup. And thoughtfully, he gave the helpful clerk a healthy tip, making Cassidy wonder if he was remembering when he'd worked two jobs to get through high school.

Back in Jake's car, Cassidy turned to Jake, ready to go wherever he chose next. "Now what?"

"My house. Since our pursuers have my tag number, it's very likely they'll be there waiting for us."

"Why don't we just go to a hotel?"

Cassidy had no fear of spending the night alone with Jake. In fact, she'd feel better if he would hold her through the dark hours, because she doubted her ability to sleep. How could she close her eyes when her safe environment had suddenly become populated with strangers who wanted to harm her? And what made it all so bewildering and frightening was that she had no idea why.

"I want to sneak up on them if they show. Figure out who they are," Jake explained with patience.

Yesterday her life had been ordinary. She'd awakened, eaten breakfast and gone to work like the rest of the world. In the space of twenty-four hours, her home had been invaded, and she'd been threatened, almost killed.

And that man, now with a partner or employee, was still after her. How had they followed her to the restaurant? Despite the police at her home, had someone been watching, waiting for her to leave?

A shiver shimmied down her spine, and the hair on her neck stood on end. What would have happened if Jake hadn't eluded those men back at the restaurant? Would she once again be tied to a chair, facing an inquisition and helpless because she didn't have the right answers?

"Jake?"

"Yes, Sunshine?"

Cassidy fought to keep her voice even. "How are we going to find out who's after me? And why."

"Maybe Harrison's trace of that call will give us a clue." Jake turned off the highway and into his neighborhood. "Maybe the crime team will find evidence at your home that will nail the guy."

Cassidy frowned. "But he wore gloves. There won't be fingerprints."

"Clues can often come from both strange and very ordinary places. Maybe one of your neighbors down the street caught the car's license plate. Or maybe he left a footprint outside or a hair on your floor. The only problem with DNA evidence is that it takes weeks to come back from the labs and it's useless without a match. And normally, the police aren't willing to share their evidence with a P.I.''

Cassidy shoved her hair off her forehead and sat up straighter. "I think we need to go through the information in the box more carefully. All the problems started with my phone call."

"Good idea."

Cassidy couldn't decide whether or not Jake was humoring her. He looked so serious and spoke as if his mind were a thousand miles away. But his eyes moved back and forth, scanning the scenery and checking the rearview mirror with a wariness that revealed he remained alert.

He noticed her fidgeting. "It's going to be okay."

Something in the deep timbre of his voice made her realize Jake was much more comfortable with the prospect of someone hunting them than she was. When she thought of detective work at all, she thought of stakeouts, picture-taking with a telephoto lens and lots of digging through computer files to find hidden information.

"You've had problems like this before?" she asked.

Jake kept his tone light as if he wasn't truly worried. "You never know when an angry ex-husband might show up ready to blast me away because I found the assets he'd thought were hidden from his wife."

"Is that mostly what you do?" Cassidy was curious how he spent his days. And his nights.

"I specialize in finding missing persons."

That piece of information shouldn't have surprised her. Jake had started looking for his sisters the day he graduated from high school. Clearly he'd become good enough to make a fine living at it. She realized that he'd diverted her worries about danger by answering her questions yet keeping the details to himself.

Jake had never been gregarious, but he'd grown up to be a regular clam. She wondered if he had any close male friends. Or, for that matter, a lady friend.

"What happens after we check at your house?"

"We hole up somewhere safe for the night."

"Will anyone mind us spending the night together?"

He drilled her with a stare, then shook his head.

"There's no hotshot lady detective after the boss?" she teased.

Jake shrugged. "I only employ men."

"Not even a secretary?"

"My detectives answer their own calls. I believe in personalized service."

"You sure you haven't turned into a male chauvinist?"

"You know better." He cocked a haughty brow. "No woman has ever applied for a job, but if one was qualified, I'd hire her in an instant. Good employees are hard to find."

So were good men. But Cassidy kept that thought to herself. Over the years she'd dated on and off. She'd had one serious relationship in college, another during law school, but neither had worked out. Lately she'd had more fun going out with her girlfriends than dates she'd been on with men.

Leaning back in the car, she looked forward to a long hot shower and maybe some mindless television to help take her thoughts off the day.

Can't you do better than that? Her conscience was back.

Better than what?

You're going to spend the night with a man who saved your life and then tenderly held you in his arms. A single available hunk, and all you can wish for is mindless television?

This is business.

What would it hurt to throw in a little monkey business on the side?

We're just friends.

There was no point considering that there could be more. Jake's mind was on finding his sisters. She suspected that as soon as they checked out his house and then arrived at a hotel, they'd reexamine the photos and read his mother's diaries and the aging documents for clues as to who might be after them.

Beside her, Jake's shoulders drew taut behind the wheel and he growled a curse. He hung a smooth right and turned four blocks before he reached his house.

"What's wrong?" Cassidy asked, her heart thumping. Craning her neck toward Jake's house, she saw a van parked across from his driveway and another dark vehicle next to it.

"I was hoping I was wrong and that no one would show up at my house. But those vehicles don't belong to my neighbors."

In an effort to sound reasonable and keep her pulse from pounding Cassidy suggested, ''Maybe they have company.''

''They don't. Someone's waiting for us.''

Chapter Four

After the day she'd had, Cassidy wasn't about to argue any further with Jake about his suspicions. Especially when he'd anticipated their pursuers showing up here. Erring on the side of safety was fine with her. Maybe the van parked across the street from Jake's home was innocent.

But maybe her pursuer had traced Jake's tag and knew he was helping her. The police-department records might indicate that Jake was protecting Cassidy. And they'd been seen together at the restaurant. It wasn't too much of a stretch for those men to have traced Jake's address from his car's plates.

Before Cassidy could ask Jake what he planned to do now, he pulled over and parked. Jake's neighborhood of wealthy homes, glass houses hidden behind high walls and locked gates, fronted the bay. But even the homes across the street from those on the water had imposing grandeur. An owl hooted ominously. Oak trees, their branches stretching over the street like grasping tentacles, cast eerie shadows.

Despite the balmy night air, goose bumps rose

along Cassidy's arms. "Why are we stopping so far away from your house?"

"It pays to be careful." He leaned over and she got a whiff of his aftershave as he opened the glove compartment and popped the trunk. She found the scent enticing and almost ran her hand along his chin, but caught herself before she'd started the motion. What had gotten into her? She must still be more shaken than she'd thought. Jake was a friend. She didn't think of him in a way that prompted impulsive caresses.

When he exited the car, she followed him to the back of the vehicle, careful to keep her distance and avoid the chance of an accidental touch. She didn't need her thoughts clouded with conflicting feelings about Jake. She liked thinking of him as the big brother she'd never had, not as a man whose face she yearned to touch just for the sheer pleasure of it.

His roomy car trunk, crammed with electronic gear and camera equipment, had enough inventory to stock a store. Jake reached for a belt with loops that held binoculars, pliers, a two-way radio and other gear she couldn't readily identify.

Jake clipped a radio to her waist, wound a wire up her back and bent the end piece over her shoulder, so the microphone rested near her mouth. "This will allow us to keep in touch."

The idea of being left alone while he went off to investigate left her cold and hollow inside. She unclipped the radio and handed it back to him. "I'm staying right next to you."

With a shrug of resignation, he handed her a hat. "Hide your hair, Sunshine. I don't intend for anyone to see us, and when your hair catches the light, it glitters like gold.''

So much for compliments. Cassidy didn't care. She simply obeyed his instructions, gathering her hair into a ponytail, then twisting it up and under the hat.

She looked from Jake toward his house down the street. ''Exactly what are we after?''

''Information.''

''What kind of information?'' she pressed.

''The useful kind.''

Well, that was helpful. She smothered her annoyance, fearful he would use any excuse to leave her behind. With Jake, she never quite knew what he was thinking. Although he was methodical, he could be unpredictable. Cassidy no more wanted to stand around in the dark alone than she wanted to play amateur detective. Still, she'd much rather accompany Jake and keep her mind occupied than wait for him. Alone.

When Jake's phone rang again, she nearly jumped out of her sneakers.

''Yes?'' Jake answered, and she saw him switch the phone to vibrate so the ring wouldn't alert anyone when they made their foray.

Jake hung up without saying another word. But his demeanor changed, becoming more stealthy, more focused, and she hesitated even to whisper a question. But she summoned the courage. She had to know what was going on and couldn't hope that Jake would volunteer the information.

''Well?''

''Harrison's friend traced the phone number.''

''And?'' she prodded.

''The number belongs to a corporation that's a subsidiary of a subsidiary.''

Cassidy understood the difficulty from her business-law courses. Corporations could hide ownership behind legal entities. If the corporation went to extremes and registered offshore, in places like the Cayman Islands or the Bahamas, it was unlikely ownership could be traced back to an individual at all.

Jake handed her a flashlight that was weighted and surprisingly heavy. Cassidy gripped the handle tightly and hefted it, trying to adjust to the weight in her hand.

''Don't turn it on. Use it as a weapon if you must. Choose your target carefully. Remember, you may only get one strike. Go for the throat, the knees or the temple.'' His blunt instructions spread the goose bumps up her arms to her shoulders and down her back. ''However, it shouldn't be necessary to defend yourself. I don't intend to get that close.''

A tight grip on the flashlight and the weight of the weapon actually gave her courage. Jake closed the trunk with a soft click, then headed down the concrete sidewalk at an easy pace. When they rounded a neighbor's yard, a dog started to bark. Lights came on in the house, and while Cassidy held her breath, the owners called the dog inside.

Meanwhile, Jake skirted the streetlights and kept to the shadows. He stopped several blocks from his house, taking cover behind garbage cans set out for the next morning's pickup. Cassidy had never realized that detective work could be so smelly. But she soon forgot the foul odors as she watched Jake work.

First he took from his belt what must be night-vision binoculars. For several long minutes, he stood without moving, his sheer presence dominating the space around him while he simply watched the street.

From her crouched position, Cassidy could see no movement. The neighbors appeared tucked nice and safe inside their two-story beachfront houses, totally unaware of the thugs parked on their street.

Headlights suddenly lit up the street like a stage. A police car rolled closer.

Jake ducked deeper into the shadows, and Cassidy, feeling like a criminal, wondered if it was necessary to hide from the cops.

Jake didn't move a muscle, and she marveled at his control. Nose itching, she fought back a sneeze. She made herself hold still despite the mosquito buzzing by her ear, the light sweat popping out on her brow and the nasty aroma taunting her nose. She tried to focus on the soft wash of waves on the shoreline and the occasional stray whiff of a salty breeze, instead of the man crouching next to her.

But she didn't succeed. Jake was so close, his warm breath brushed her cheek. His shadow engulfed hers. And she had to restrain herself from reaching over to take his hand. These impulses to touch him kept coming out of nowhere. Having so little control over herself made her uneasy.

Finally the police car turned onto the next street. And while it took her eyes minutes to readjust to the darkness, she realized Jake didn't have that problem. He'd either looked away from the bright lights or had closed his eyes.

He'd replaced the night-vision binoculars with an odd-looking camera. As he loaded film, she heard a soft whirring sound. Then a series of clicks as Jake took at least a dozen pictures.

Probably only five minutes had passed before they left and returned to his car, but it seemed like hours. Although Cassidy's mouth was dry from the tension, she could no longer keep back her questions as Jake once more began to drive, first out of the subdivision, then onto the freeway, heading north.

"Did you get anything good?"

He shrugged.

"Well, what did you see?"

"Not much. But the camera lens is more sensitive than the human eye. I'm hoping once the pictures are developed that we'll get something useful."

Cassidy rested her head against the plush leather seat, unwilling to ask more questions. She had no idea where he was taking her, but he seemed to have a destination in mind.

Exhaustion was finally taking its toll. She'd started early this morning—cleaned the attic, confronted Jake, suffered a man breaking and entering her home and almost killing her, and now all she wanted was to close her eyes, preferably in a comfortable bed, and sleep.

She wondered if she was trusting Jake too much. But he seemed so competent that he inspired her trust. In her youth, she had always relied on him to do the right thing, and her past feelings for him reinforced that confidence now. Tomorrow, when she could think more clearly, she'd reevaluate her situation. She'd think better after a good night of rest.

She must have fallen asleep, because when she

awoke she was startled by the change in temperature. It was much cooler here, wherever "here" was.

Jake had opened her car door and shaken her awake. "Come on, Sunshine. A bed's waiting for you."

Cassidy glanced at the clock and realized they'd been driving for more than an hour. A crescent moon shone down on a pasture surrounded by hills. Crickets chirped, and frogs made so much racket she had trouble hearing herself think. While most of Florida was flat, the state did have a few hilly areas. Here the air smelled of pine. Up ahead an inviting A-frame cotage nestled on the shore of a small lake.

"Where are we?"

"Brooksville. My firm keeps a cabin here to hide clients when their safety's at stake."

Cassidy knew she should ask whose name the cabin was in, but she just couldn't wrap her tongue around the words. Without Jake's help, she might not have had the energy to stand. She revived slightly in the nippy air on the short walk from the car to the cabin. Mostly she just enjoyed the security of Jake's arm around her and concentrated on placing one foot in front of the other.

The cabin, simple in design, a living-room-and-kitchen combination facing the lake with a bedroom and bath in the back, was decorated with simple pine furnishings that needed little care. The oak floor and hewn beams overhead gave the place a rugged masculine appeal.

"You'll find a toothbrush, soap and shampoo in the bathroom, and a robe in the closet. Help yourself to any clothing you can find that fits." He must have read the questions in her eyes. "We aren't the first people to use this cabin after being on the run. The kitchen's stocked with canned goods, the freezer with meat."

Cassidy took one look at the immaculate bedroom and decided to bathe first, then sleep. While Jake started a fire in the living area, she took advantage of the shower. Helping herself to shampoo and cream rinse, she washed her hair twice.

The bathroom lacked a hair dryer, so she slipped on the robe and twisted a towel into a turban over her hair. After washing her underwear and hanging it up to dry, she rejoined Jake. She found him squatting in front of the fire, poking a log, but mostly just staring at the flames. Firelight flickered over his features, and she wondered what he was thinking. He seemed a million miles away.

Tucking her bare legs beneath her, she sat on a battered couch, its leather soft as warm caramel. "A penny for your thoughts."

Jake stared into the flames for so long she didn't think he'd answer. The fire pushed back the darkness and lent an air of intimacy to the room. An intimacy that only she seemed aware of.

For a big man, Jake could hold himself remarkably still. Yet his whiskey-colored eyes always shined with intensity. The startling combination of stillness and suppressed emotion held her mesmerized. She wondered if she'd ever really known him.

But if she hadn't, why did she feel safer just being in his presence?

Jake dusted off his hands and came to his feet with the grace of an athlete. "I think I'll wash up."

She suddenly recalled her lingerie hanging in the shower and her cheeks heated. Tired, accustomed to living alone, she hadn't thought through their living accommodations and that they'd be sharing the bathroom.

Quickly she rose from her perch and bumped into Jake. He reached out to steady her, and she jerked back. "I rinsed out my...I left..."

He smiled at her then, a smile that filled those golden eyes with amusement and held a special place in her memories. "I've seen your underwear before, Sunshine."

The moment he referred to suddenly came rushing back. Winters in Florida might be wonderfully temperate, but August nights could be stiflingly hot. She recalled meeting Jake in the park after a suffocating heat-filled day where the temperature had soared over a hundred. Darkness later that evening hadn't helped to relieve the stifling heat.

Cassidy's hair had stuck to her head and lay hot and heavy over her shoulders and down her back. Her damp clothes had clung to her, and not even eating ice cream had cooled her off. It was a night they should have been inside with the air-conditioning blasting. But Jake hadn't been able to afford to turn on his air, and Cassidy had known how uncomfortable Jake felt at her home.

So they'd walked to the community pool, climbed the fence and swum in their underwear. Other kids might have skinny-dipped, but Cassidy had had her dream of going to college and law school firmly in her mind. She wouldn't let herself become emotionally involved or let their relationship go beyond friendship. But even then, she'd trusted Jake to know how she felt about him, how she considered him a best friend.

She grinned at the memory. "I'd forgotten that night. We were lucky we weren't caught and arrested."

"Yeah."

It wasn't sarcasm in his voice but regret and something else that Cassidy couldn't quite read. Before she could catch the look in his eyes, Jake turned away from her and headed to the shower.

Without him, the room seemed larger and colder. Cassidy put another log on the fire, then checked the lock on the door and the windows. Outside, the clouds shaded the moon and a fog rolled in. The frogs' croaking had died down and the crickets seemed to be sleeping. She searched for rain clouds, but the night sky looked cloudless. The entire state was going through a drought, and they desperately needed rain.

Cassidy found a blanket in a closet and floated it over her lap as she resumed her place on the sofa. Closing her eyes, she still saw Jake. Imagined him in the shower, the water sluicing over his dark hair and broad shoulders. What was wrong with her? She didn't think of him as the boy she'd once known but the man he'd become, the man she found more attractive than she would have liked. The man she kept wanting to touch.

Cassidy tried thinking of Jake as a brother, but disturbing images, sexy images, kept getting in the way. Thoughts of him as a man with wants and needs and desires disturbed her. Luckily when she'd told Jake she wished they'd kept in touch, he'd seemed to sense that she'd spoken from a combination of nostalgia and insecurities and friendship. But had she?

Suddenly Cassidy wondered what it would be like to make love to a man like Jake. Even as a kid, Jake Cochran would have been gentle—he wouldn't have laughed at her inexperience.

A loud bang startled Cassidy from her thoughts. She sat up with a gasp, the blanket falling to the floor, her heart pumping wildly.

Had someone banged on the door? Had someone found them? Had she seen the doorknob turn?

Rushing to the window, she peered through the darkness toward the lake. She'd just about convinced herself she'd dreamed the noise when the bald head of a man appeared, his face wild-eyed, with horn-rimmed glasses and bushy brows, two inches from the windowpane.

Cassidy screamed and headed straight for the bathroom. And Jake.

A very wet, very naked Jake.

JAKE HEARD HER SCREAM and his throat tightened. Grabbing his gun from the shoulder holster hanging over the towel rack, he sprinted from the bathroom, his only fear for Cassidy's safety. When he'd almost lost her earlier today, he'd realized how much she still meant to him. But now that she was in his protection, her safety was his responsibility.

Expecting to meet trouble, he banged, instead, into a terrified Cassidy. Her eyes looked too big in a face that was pale. Something had scared her, and without thinking, he shoved her behind him. Then he raised his weapon, searching the room for danger.

He didn't see anyone.

"There's a man outside," Cassidy whispered, her voice trembling. "I saw him through the window."

"Who?"

"A man."

"What did he look like?"

"Wild. He looked mad and wild. And he wore horn-rimmed glasses."

Before Cassidy could say more, someone banged on the front door. The doorknob turned as someone tested the lock.

"Damn it, Cochran," the very familiar voice of Harrison demanded, "open the door already. I'm exposed out here."

With a measure of relief, Jake lowered his weapon and yanked open the front door. Harrison took one look at Jake's wet naked body and shook his head. "I see I'm not the only one exposed."

"Cassidy Atkins, this is my partner, Harrison Gordon." Jake motioned his friend and employee inside. "What took you so long?"

Behind him, Cassidy gasped in surprise and anger. "You were expecting him?"

Jake immediately realized his mistake. He should have told Cassidy that Harrison would be meeting them. She had every right to be angry with him, and he knew his explanation sounded weak and sheepish. But in his defense, he wasn't accustomed to making explanations to clients. "You were sleeping when I asked Harrison to meet us and bring me some things."

Cassidy turned on Jake, her eyes still sparking with fury. "Suppose I'd shot him?"

"I didn't give you a gun, Sunshine."

"That's beside the point. If he'd come in, I would have attacked him. And it would have been all your fault."

Jake eyed her. No doubt she didn't know what to do with the adrenaline racing through her from her scare. Cassidy hadn't seemed to listen to his explanation. He was about to speak again when he noticed that she was busy trying to look anywhere but at him. And not succeeding. Was that mirth overtaking her former fear?

Jake finally realized he was standing in the living room in the buff, a gun in his hand, dripping water on the floor. "If you don't mind, I'll go finish my shower."

He retreated with as much dignity as a man with no clothes on could muster. He heard Cassidy giggle and Harrison roar with laughter.

He returned to the living room ten minutes later to find Cassidy and Harrison ensconced on the sofa, talking softly. Harrison stood and wiped his lenses clean of fog. "I was just telling Cassidy that I've traced the license number you gave me."

Cassidy glared at Jake, probably because he hadn't told her he'd seen the license number through the night-vision binoculars. He'd wanted to find out exactly who they were dealing with first, but Harrison had scuttled that plan by confiding in her.

Somehow Cassidy always had a way of casting order into disorder. Normally Jake and Harrison worked on the same wavelength, explanations between them unnecessary. Jake was rarely as annoyed with Harrison as he was right now, and he had no one to blame but himself. Still, without being told, Harrison usually understood that Jake didn't share information with a client as if she was a partner. But Cassidy had a way of getting under the skin and finding out what she wanted to know. Jake supposed he couldn't blame his friend. Not when she affected him exactly the same way.

"So who are the plates registered to?" Jake asked as he wiped up the water he'd dripped on the floor with a towel.

"Dr. Brian Duncan."

"A doctor?" Jake frowned. The name didn't ring any bells, and he knew many of the area's street criminals. "You checked this Duncan out?"

"Sure did. He reported the stolen vehicle earlier today. The guy's a veterinarian."

Cassidy looked from Harrison to Jake, confusion in her eyes. "What does this mean?"

"That the guys who are after you are pros," Harrison told her without hesitation. "They're watching our office. I had a difficult time shaking a tail on the way here."

Cassidy reacted with a slight widening of her eyes, a flaring of her nostrils and an obvious effort not to show her fear. But her lips tightened into a thin line, and Jake knew that inside she was trembling.

Jake glared at Harrison for scaring Cassidy, and the man shrugged and took another opportunity to wipe his glasses.

Cassidy caught the byplay between the two men and sighed. "Jake, keeping me in the dark isn't going to protect me. I need to know what's going on without your trying to second-guess how I'll take bad news."

"Fine," Jake agreed, having no intention of telling her more than she needed to know. He had a bad feeling about this case. The response time from whoever was after Cassidy and possibly him was too fast, too slick, not to have him really worried for her safety.

Cassidy eyed Jake as if she knew he was patronizing her. No doubt he'd have to defend himself from her charges later.

From his pocket Jake dug the film used for taking pictures of the vehicle in front of his house and tossed it to Harrison. "Have this developed and see what you can come up with."

Harrison plucked the film out of the air, juggled it, then shoved it into a front pocket that already bulged with pens, business cards and phone messages.

"I suppose you aren't going to tell me if you find anything on that film, either," Cassidy complained. "I thought we had this settled. Either you share the information with me, or I find another private investigator."

"The lady knows how to bargain," Harrison said with a glint in his warm brown eyes that suggested he was enjoying Jake's discomfort.

Jake ignored Harrison, instead reading the determination in the set of Cassidy's chin, the hardening of her eyes, and nodded, this time meaning it. "When Harrison calls, you'll be the first to know."

"There's more," Harrison said, and from his tone, Jake knew he wouldn't like what his friend said next. Especially since he hadn't asked Harrison to check out any other clues.

They really had little to go on.

"You found out who owned the subsidiary belonging to the company Cassidy called?" Jake asked.

"I'm still digging. But I'm not hopeful. The trail is too well hidden. These guys are good. They don't make mistakes."

"Everyone makes mistakes," Jake muttered. Including him. He'd made the biggest mistake of all by getting involved with Cassidy again. He couldn't seem to think clearly with her around. When she told him she'd missed him, she'd affected him in a way he couldn't combat, because she slipped by his weaknesses—which annoyed the hell out of him.

How could he protect her when his mind kept drifting? How could he concentrate when she looked at him and told him she'd missed him? Even now he was wondering what she'd meant by that remark when he should have been asking Harrison what else he had.

"What more did you find out?" Cassidy asked, her shoulders squared, her back straight as if bracing for more bad news.

"Jake's house and office phones are bugged. So is the phone at your house."

Chapter Five

Cassidy heard Harrison tell Jake about the bugged phones. Maybe it was her exhaustion, maybe it was that her mind couldn't take another setback, but she just couldn't think anymore about all this detective stuff. She didn't even like *reading* mysteries, much less figuring them out. She preferred romance novels, especially ones that made her laugh or cry.

So she had difficulty thinking about telephone bugs and stolen license plates when she could dwell on far more pleasant topics. Such as running smack-dab into a naked Jake Cochran.

Whew! He sure was built. The sleek tailored clothes he wore hid broad shoulders and a powerful chest covered with a triangle of dark curls. Slender hips, muscular thighs and calves. And the cutest tightest butt she'd ever seen.

She refused to think about his sex, nestled in more dark curls. She absolutely, positively wouldn't think about it. She'd always hated women who inventoried body parts. She would never do such a thing.

So who practically salivated at seeing him naked?

Well, *she* had. She had been cataloging each asset,

her mouth almost watering over the sum total of his parts. The man looked good in clothes. But naked, he was like a Greek sculpture.

Still, what the hell was wrong with her? This was Jake she was thinking about. A friend. She didn't think of Jake as a potential lover.

You just did.

Hush.

You're lying to yourself if you can't admit he's got the most perfect—

"Shut up." When the room suddenly fell silent and Jake and Harrison looked at her curiously, Cassidy realized she'd spoken aloud. "Sorry, I was arguing with myself."

"Who won?" Jake teased.

I did, her conscience replied smugly. *You'll never think of him as a brother again.*

Cassidy blushed and stood. "It's been a long day. Maybe I should turn in."

Harrison rose to his feet, too. He handed Jake three cell phones and a leather bag filled with what looked like more electronics equipment.

"Keep in touch." Harrison shook Cassidy's hand goodbye. "Sorry I frightened you, ma'am." Then he turned to Jake. "There's a shoe box of cash in that bag, so don't go leaving it unattended."

After Harrison departed, Jake locked the door. For the first time Cassidy realized the cabin had only one bedroom, one bed. And Jake was much too tall to sleep comfortably on the sofa. "Jake, I fit on the couch better than you do. You take the bed."

He shook his head, rubbing a kink from his shoulder. "I doubt I'll sleep tonight. You might as well be comfortable."

She planted her hands on her hips. "You need sleep just as much as I do. If tomorrow is anything like today, you'll need to be alert to protect me." She hesitated, then blurted, "We're both adults. There's no reason we can't share the bed."

Attagirl. Now you're talking.

Would you please go back to wherever you came from? Cassidy begged.

You want me to leave when your life is finally getting interesting?

Yes!

Cassidy caught Jake looking at her oddly. She wondered if she moved her lips when she talked to herself. She'd better be careful. She'd had a hard enough time convincing him to let her stay with him. If he started to doubt her mental health, he'd insist she hole up someplace he considered safer.

"I want to look through my mother's diaries and at the photographs again before I turn in." Jake had avoided discussing their sleeping arrangements, and Cassidy knew if he slept at all, he fully intended to use the couch. She kept forgetting how stubborn Jake could be and how easily he avoided conflict by deflecting the issue. As sleepy as she felt, Cassidy knew she couldn't lie down and sleep while Jake went through his mother's things alone. An obligation to support him in any way she could overrode her sleepiness.

Especially when she looked into Jake's eyes. They looked haunted with betrayal, and the fact that he seemed to try so hard to hide his pain from her made her heart go out to him.

"Jake?"

"Yeah?"

"What has you so worried?" she asked as she refused the comfortable couch and searched through the kitchen for coffee and two mugs.

Jake raked a hand through his hair. "As much as I'd like to believe our problems are due to one of my old cases or one of your clients, the facts don't add up. Your phone call triggered someone to come after you and me. I can't see any other alternative but to believe that there's something in the box that they want."

She found coffee in the refrigerator and started a pot. While she rinsed the dust from two mugs, she frowned. "Why would anyone want that old stuff? Who would think it valuable except your mother's children?"

"I don't know. But Harrison checked my phone messages, and apparently the clerk I tipped called my house and said two guys came into the print shop after we left. They flashed official-looking badges and asked what we copied and what we did with the copies."

Cassidy recalled Jake's tip and understood why the clerk went out of his way to tell Jake what had happened. "But you lost the tail. How did they discover we'd stopped in the print shop?"

"Good question. They must have traced my credit card, which means they have an especially good computer hacker working for them."

"What kind of badges did they flash?"

"The kid wasn't sure. He said they were silver. I suspect they were fake."

"Why?"

"Law enforcement isn't usually that efficient. Besides, we aren't criminals. Why would the law be after us?"

Cassidy plugged in the pot and added coffee and water. "How did the clerk get your phone number?"

"It was on the receipt I filled out for the parcel service. What's important is not how they did it. What I'm concerned about is my sisters."

"The mail receipts had their addresses?" she guessed, suddenly realizing why Jake was so concerned.

He nodded. "So if they can't get the information from my box of stuff, maybe they'll try and take it from my sisters." His face deepened with lines of worry.

Cassidy found sugar packets on a shelf next to non-dairy creamer. "I know you didn't want to call, but maybe you should warn them."

"Harrison and I discussed that while you slept in the car. Since I don't trust my phone not to be bugged, I stopped and called them from a pay phone. Neither sister was home. But I hired a bodyguard to protect each of them."

Cassidy could hear the frustration in his tone and could only imagine his despair. After all his years of searching for his sisters, he'd found them—only to place them in danger. The coffee she handed him seemed too small an offering for the trouble she'd brought him this morning, but Jake eagerly accepted the coffee, refusing the creamer and sugar.

"I'd go check on my sisters myself, but I might lead our pursuers right to their doors."

"Let's hope they're off on vacation or out of town for business, instead of grocery shopping or at the movies."

"Harrison will keep trying to call and warn them. Meanwhile, maybe by the time my sisters return, we can nail these guys."

"How?" Cassidy tried to keep the skepticism from her voice. While she didn't doubt Jake's ability or his determination, they didn't have much to go on.

"If we can figure out what they want, we can figure out who would want it."

"Sounds like a plan." While she added two packets of sugar to her coffee, Jake brought over his briefcase. He emptied the documents on the kitchen table while she masked a yawn.

The pictures jumped out at her, black-and-white grainy eight-by-tens. She flipped over the pictures, hoping they might be labeled, but no one had written anything on the backs. Cassidy dealt the pictures out like cards faceup in neat rows of four across and three down. All the pictures except two had people in them. One showed an island, the other a cove.

Cassidy peered at the people in the pictures. From their manner of dress and the vehicles in the street scenes, she estimated the time period to be mid to late 1960s, a few years before Jake had been born.

She peered at the people's faces for clues, wondering if Jake's features resembled his folks'. "Do you remember what your parents looked like?"

"My mom had short blond hair."

None of the women in the photos were blond. Yet

one had eyes shaped liked Jake's and long straight dark hair that hung past her waist. She was in several pictures and in one shot a tall dark-haired man with a military haircut had his arm around her. They were looking adoringly into each other's eyes.

Cassidy pointed to the pair. "Could they be your parents?"

Jake looked up from the documents he was sorting. "I just told you my mom had—"

"Hair can be cut, the color changed."

Jake picked up the photograph and stared at the couple. He remained silent for a full minute. Finally he flicked the picture back onto the table in disgust. "I just don't know."

"Don't be so hard on yourself. How old were you when you last saw your mother? Five?" When Jake didn't respond, Cassidy looked again at the picture. "The man's built like you. He's tall and has your eyes."

"Lots of men are tall and have eyes like mine."

"But he has the same silhouette, his neckline and shoulders are shaped like yours. And there's something about his smile that reminds me of you."

"You're seeing things that aren't there."

"Maybe. But your mother saved these pictures for a reason. It's likely she's in one of them. And it's also likely that your father is, too."

She could tell Jake wasn't taking her suggestions seriously. Perhaps she *was* reading too much into a look, a smile and a similarity of neck and shoulders. "Okay, Mr. Hotshot Detective, what have you found?"

Jake flipped past the birth certificates to a marriage certificate. "Now this is odd."

"What?"

"It's a marriage certificate for a Mary Lou Ellis to a Michael Scott. My mother's name was Janet, and I can't recall her maiden name. Dad was Steven Cochran."

"That is strange. Maybe it's not your parents' marriage certificate."

"Why would my mother have saved someone else's? Unless..."

"Unless what?"

"Unless they changed their names." Jake stood and paced, waving his hand as he spoke. "That would explain why I couldn't find them. I couldn't find social-security numbers, tax returns, school records. I searched for years and never found anything about Janet and Steve Cochran because they didn't exist."

"They changed their names before you were born?"

"They must have. It's the only thing that makes sense."

Cassidy frowned. "Unless my father mixed up the files and someone else's marriage certificate fell into this box."

Jake's voice held suppressed excitement. "No, it makes sense that they changed their names. It explains why I could never find a trace of them."

"But why would they do that?"

"There could be lots of reasons. They wanted to hide."

"From who?"

"An ex-lover. A parent, maybe my grandparents.

Or maybe they were falsely accused of committing a crime and had to flee.''

Cassidy could see Jake turning over the possibilities in his mind. He had quite an imagination. She couldn't have come up with so many reasons so quickly. Perhaps they should leave the past in the past. Jake might not like what he found.

Yet she had no doubt that he would find the answers. She could read the determination in the fire of his topaz eyes and hear it in the excitement in his voice. Jake wouldn't give up until he had the answers he sought, until he'd solved the mystery of his past.

But what would solving the mystery cost him? He'd never forgive himself if anything happened to his sisters. But while she and Jake were being hunted, they couldn't go to them. She was sure Jake didn't like relying on bodyguards to protect his sisters. But what other choice did they have?

Their pursuers had been remarkably organized. They'd found her within thirty minutes of her phone call. They'd staked out both their homes and businesses and bugged their phones. It was only a matter of time before they found this cabin, too.

JAKE FULLY INTENDED to work through the night for a multitude of reasons, all of them important. First off, ever since Cassidy had run into him before he'd had a chance to wrap a towel around his hips, he'd seen the speculation in her eyes. He wasn't the lanky boy she remembered. His muscles had finally caught up to his height and he'd filled out. Special Forces training had done the rest, giving his body a definition that he'd longed for as a teenager to impress the girls. Okay, to impress Cassidy.

But now he didn't want her to notice him for his physique. He wasn't sure if he wanted her to notice him at all, since he found the sexual tension that simmered between them distracting. For his sake, for her sake and for his sisters' sakes, he needed to keep his mind on the case. Lives could be at stake. The feel of this case had a gritty professionalism about it that kept him on edge. Jake would never forgive himself if lack of concentration caused someone he cared about to be hurt.

Despite his best intentions, he couldn't help feeling pleased that Cassidy found him attractive. He tried to rationalize the idea away. He knew danger made the brain increase production of certain chemicals that sometimes caused people to do things they wouldn't do under normal circumstances. Men and women often made love the night before they went to war. Kidnapping victims even fell in love with their captors.

Jake didn't want Cassidy under these circumstances. Letting her go ten years before had been too difficult. He wasn't about to take a chance for a few nights of pleasure—not when he already knew how long it would take to forget her when she returned to her normal life.

He'd learned from his past mistakes. He wouldn't repeat them. So when Cassidy walked over and put her hand on his shoulder and peered at the document he'd been holding and pretending to read for the past five minutes, he ignored the increase in his heart rate. Pretended he couldn't take in her delicious feminine scent. Faked a lack of interest in seeing if he could tug her into his lap and tease her narrowed lips into a full lushness.

"Found anything?"

"I'm not sure."

He hadn't read a word but forced himself to do so now. "A diploma. From the University of Florida for Mary Lou Ellis." He picked up another diploma. "And one for Michael Scott."

Cassidy kept her hand on his shoulder and leaned over to read them. Jake knew he should remove her hand, but he didn't want to reveal to her how much her touch disturbed him. So he shifted uncomfortably in his chair and crossed his legs, unwilling to let her glimpse the bulge in his trousers.

She drank her coffee. "Jake, I don't want you to get false hopes. The stuff I found in my father's attic was dusty and most likely had been there for over twenty years. Maybe the adoption papers for your sisters just got mixed up with another of dad's clients. This Mary Lou Ellis and Michael Scott may not have anything to do with your family at all."

Jake finally turned and took her hand off his shoulder and held it in his. "It's the only conjecture that makes sense. The reason I never found anything was because I'd searched for records under their assumed names. Not the ones they were born with."

Taking Cassidy's hand from his shoulder had been a mistake. Because now she was looking directly at him and at the same time grazing the calluses on his hand with her soft palm; the strength in her fingers reminded him why he'd fallen for her once before. The perfect combination of strength and softness, she appealed to him in ways he couldn't keep fighting.

Her willingness to help him, her courage in the face of danger, slipped beneath his resolve like spilled water seeping under a door. He couldn't keep her out, and when she stood so close, he had trouble remembering why he was resisting getting his feet wet.

As if sensing his moment of weakness, she floated onto his lap with the fluidity of a cat. And suddenly he knew he was in over his head, drowning in new scents, new sensations. He tended to forget her impulsiveness until she knocked his feet out from under him.

And then it was too late. Her curves pressed against him in all the right places, and he ached to put his arms around her and pull her into a tight embrace. But he didn't. He might not have enough fortitude to push her away, but he wouldn't encourage her, either.

Tilting back her head, she parted her lips slightly and locked gazes with him, her knowing eyes letting him see that she was thoroughly comfortable in his arms. "Tomorrow let's drive to Gainesville."

He forced himself to answer her in a casual tone, pretending that she didn't affect him, hoping his eyes didn't reflect how badly he wanted her. "The university may have records."

Her fingers traced tiny circles on the back of his neck, releasing tension along his shoulders. Her nails lightly scraped a sensitive spot near the pulse at his throat. "Maybe we can find a professor who remembers them."

He could no longer prevent his tone from deepening. How could he when she snuggled so close? Still, he kept his words on their investigation. "We can start with the registrar's office and admissions."

She seemed eager to keep talking, as if by doing so she gave him the opportunity to pretend the attraction between them wasn't extraordinary, that the simmering tension could keep building without consequences. "We can trace their former address."

She twisted until she could face him. "Find family."

"Neighbors."

"Someone who can..."

Jake heard the words, but he was more fascinated by the temptation of her lips. He wouldn't kiss her. He wouldn't think about her firm bottom pressed against his thighs. Her breast nestled against the crook of his arm. He wouldn't take advantage of her need to be held. He wasn't going to kiss her even if her lips were only inches from his.

As if sensing his resolve, Cassidy allowed a tiny smile to escape. She turned back to him and impulsively wound her arms around his neck, taking him by surprise.

Her mouth, a mere inch from his, tantalized him. "Now where were we?"

She moved slowly, sensuously, giving him every opportunity to pull away. But as if mesmerized by the heated glimmer in her eyes, he held perfectly still, neither advancing nor retreating, simply leaving her with all the choices.

And she chose to taunt him.

He figured that within a moment, impetuous Cassidy would kiss him. But she was in no hurry. Instead, she explored his face with her fingertips, the pads of her fingertips circling the lobes of his ears, his forehead and eyebrows and the bridge of his nose. Her delicate touch brewed a storm of needs inside him. Not just physical needs, but emotional turmoil.

Cassidy hadn't simply been his first teenage crush. She'd been his first real friend. And back then, as much as he'd wanted to take their relationship to the next level, he'd known he would have lost her friendship if he'd tried. She'd make it very clear that she thought having deeper feelings for any man would jeopardize her resolve to follow her dreams.

But she meant everything to him. All his life Jake had longed for a family. A wife. Kids. He now possessed a house with a three-car garage, but he still ached for a family, for a woman to tend the home, take care of the kids and be waiting for him after a hard day of investigation. Cassidy didn't fit into this picture. Cassidy was a career woman.

Yet just because she was the wrong woman for him, he couldn't so easily put his feelings for her aside. She'd been the first person who'd cared about him since he was five and had lost his parents. And now here she was sitting on his lap, her head tilted back with that lion's mane of hair still damp and enveloping him in a sensual haze.

"Sunshine, maybe we should talk about—"

"I don't want to talk. I just want to feel," Cassidy murmured, her voice husky and sultry and very sure of itself.

"But—"

"Time for talking is over." She raised her lips halfway to his. "Kiss me."

He didn't know if he dipped his head or she raised hers. But their lips met, and he couldn't hold back the flood of desire that crashed over him. Not when she parted her lips under his, yielding to him, tasting sweeter than any drift of spun sugar. She was all woman, fire and lightning and temptation and pure heaven rolled into one.

She didn't hold any part of herself back. Like a wave building and cresting before rolling and dashing itself onto the shore, Cassidy kissed him with a fervor that matched the soaring of his spirit.

Jake finally came up for air and out of his daze to realize she'd kissed him with her eyes wide open. Dilated with passion, tinged with a heavy-lidded sensuality, her eyes challenged him to take more. He knew she was about to ask him to make love to her. And he wanted to. But he couldn't let her ask and then refuse her.

With more determination than he'd ever exhibited in his life, Jake pulled back. "We shouldn't."

She nibbled a spot on his neck. "Why not?"

"Because I don't do one-night stands," he growled, his voice harsh with his frustration. He never should have kissed her or allowed her to kiss him. He'd known better. And now he would pay the price—sleepless nights, dreams of what could have been, memories that would haunt his waking hours. But as much as it would cost him now to refuse her, if he made love to her, he didn't think he'd ever be able to let her go.

"That's what I am to you, a one-night stand?"

"What else could you be?" he lied to protect himself. She was far more. But even so, he had enough sense to realize she didn't love him. She wanted a night of pleasure with someone safe, someone to chase away her loneliness and fears. Well, Jake had too much self-respect to let her use him.

"You're trying to push me away, start a fight," she murmured as she tried to kiss him again.

If he let her, he'd be a goner for sure. She was very good at reading him. But he needed to keep a smidgen of self-respect.

Jake held her shoulders firmly, refusing to let her change his mind. She'd already done enough damage with her kiss. "Think anything you like, Sunshine. Just leave me the hell alone."

Chapter Six

Cassidy fought past the sensual haze Jake's kiss had woven around her, tried to understand his words. He'd just told her to leave him alone, but his body made him a liar. She was too close not to see his pupils dilate with need. Too close not to hear his ragged breaths between words. Too close not to feel a very interested part of his anatomy denying what he'd just said.

Hurt and confusion had mixed as he'd pushed her away. And the reasons behind his harsh words left her wondering why he didn't just tell her what was going on. Obviously he found her attractive. He'd kissed her with a passion that had rocked her to her core. Cassidy wasn't innocent. Yet never before had a kiss made her feel intoxicated, bubbly with the happiness of being alive, excited to be held, and happy to give and receive affection.

And Jake had said he didn't want her.

His words told her so. His hands on her shoulders kept her from leaning against him. Cassidy raised her chin, looked directly into Jake's eyes, which were filled with an edgy heat that contradicted the fierce expression on his face.

Without another word, she slipped off his lap, walked to the bedroom and lay down on the bed. She'd left the door open, knowing he'd never walk through it.

Cassidy laced her fingers behind her head and stared at the ceiling in the darkness. Their kiss had been stunningly passionate. It had made her forget the danger they were in. She'd forgotten the reason she was here. She'd simply let taste and touch and smell take over, and it had been better than reading her romances. Better than her dreams. Better than any hot-fudge sundae—her consolation dessert when a date didn't turn out so hot.

But Jake's kiss had been hotter than a Fourth of July bottle rocket. And he'd sent her soaring farther than she'd ever expected to go.

Then after showing her exactly how good it could be, he'd pushed her away. Was it simply him being able to control his hormones? She didn't have the courage to go back into that room and ask him. Not with her lips still swollen and tender from his kiss and her breasts aching for his touch. Certainly not until Jake could speak in a rational tone of voice. His last demand to keep away from him had been close to a growl.

Which only proved that the kiss had affected him, too. Cassidy couldn't fathom the reason for the contradiction between his words and his actions. She expected to spend a sleepless night pondering the peculiarities of the male species. And one male in particular. But it had been a very long exhausting day.

Sometime during the next hour, her eyes drifted closed and she slept.

Someone was rocking her. Jake?

She opened her eyes to sunlight. Cassidy almost always awakened with full use of all her faculties. She didn't need coffee to jump-start her day, but came awake, totally aware and refreshed.

"Rise and shine. We've got a long day ahead of us," Jake told her from the safety of the bathroom. He'd already shaved and showered. "It's all yours." He gestured to the bathroom as he sauntered out.

So he planned to act as if that kiss had never happened. Cassidy might have thought she'd dreamed it, but the details were too vivid in her mind. Jake had the most wonderful masculine scent, kind of musky and earthy. Coffee on his lips had flavored the memory so that she doubted she'd ever drink another cup without thinking of Jake and that kiss.

Cassidy smelled bacon frying and hurried to check the closet for clothes. She found nothing suitable. At least the underwear she'd rinsed out last night had dried. After her shower, she slipped them back on under the clothes she'd worn the day before, thinking that a shopping trip was in order.

When she joined Jake in the main room, bright sunlight gleamed through the cabin's windows, and the room had lost the intimacy of last night. Jake had set the table. A glass of orange juice sat next to a plate that held a Belgian waffle. Jake was transferring crisp bacon from the frying pan onto her plate when she joined him.

"Looks great." She took a seat, placed a napkin on her lap and waited for Jake to join her after he poured them both coffee. Cassidy added creamer to hers and watched the dairy product disappear into a cloud of murky darkness. Just like that kiss would vanish if she didn't bring it up. Instinctively she knew Jake wouldn't. And Cassidy wasn't sure she had the courage to ask Jake why he'd pushed her away. Suppose he gave her an answer she didn't want to hear? Maybe it would be better not to mention the kiss, either.

She sipped her coffee, trying to make up her mind, when Jake pulled out a map. He bit into a slice of bacon as he traced a red line. "If we take the highway east to I 75 north, we can be in Gainesville before lunch."

"I need to stop at a store and pick up a few things." Cassidy caught the reluctance in his eyes but wouldn't take no for an answer. "Harrison brought you clothes. I need some, too. And I'm a quick shopper."

"Fine."

With that settled, they both finished their breakfast and cleaned up the cabin while making small talk. Cassidy used Jake's newest cell phone to call her secretary and instruct her that she wouldn't be in for the rest of the week. Next she called a colleague and asked her to take over a few hours of free counseling at the women's clinic. Luckily Cassidy had no pets to care for, no swimming pool that needed chemicals. Her lawn and plants might suffer because she couldn't be there to water them, but that couldn't be helped. She'd re-sod and replant if necessary, although she might have to wait until rainy season.

They walked outside and Cassidy was surprised to

see that the Mercedes they'd driven yesterday was gone. A white four-wheel-drive SUV was parked there, instead. "Harrison's doing?" she guessed.

"Standard operating procedure." Jake swung his bag into the rear compartment. He stowed the briefcase with his mother's legacy next to the driver's seat. "Whoever is after us saw us in the Mercedes. This one isn't even registered to the firm."

Recalling her question about the cabin's ownership, Cassidy slipped into the passenger seat and buckled her seat belt. "Can the deed on the cabin be traced back to you?"

"Not easily." Jake started the engine. "But eventually, yes. That's why I'm anxious to get out of here."

Jake stopped at a twenty-four-hour superstore, and Cassidy loaded up on clothes, toiletries and a backpack in which to carry everything. After using an automated teller machine to withdraw her daily limit, she moved to the checkout line. Her shopping didn't take as long as getting through the cashier's line, and it seemed longer because of a man who stood behind her. He seemed too interested in her, but every time she looked up, he turned the other way. Nervous, she returned to Jake and the SUV.

She waited until Jake pulled out of the parking lot to voice her concern. "Are you sure those men followed us to the print shop after you used a credit card?"

"It's possible they planted a bug on my car in the restaurant parking lot."

"You think so?" Hope rose inside her. If Jake was

correct, then they should be safe in the new car Harrison had brought them.

"It's not difficult to get hold of a bug and tracking device. Between the Internet and magazine classified advertisements, anyone could order one."

"But?"

"Having one and planting it shows an extraordinary amount of forethought."

Cassidy finally asked the question that had been bothering her ever since she'd paid cash for her purchase. "How difficult is it to track ATM withdrawals?"

"The equipment's sophisticated and way beyond the means of most criminals." Jake frowned, clearly thinking hard. "But a good computer hacker could probably do it. Why?"

Her heartbeat accelerated. "I thought someone might have followed me inside the store—I paid in cash, but I used the ATM."

"No one could have traced an ATM withdrawal and shown up within just a few minutes."

"It might be my imagination running wild."

"Maybe not. Harrison claims he lost his tail before he arrived at the cabin, but they might have picked us up as we drove into town."

"Wouldn't that take a lot of planning? Like from some big organization such as the FBI?"

"Maybe."

Cassidy frowned. "You told me that the clerk at the print shop said the two guys flashed FBI official-looking badges at him. Could they have been FBI?"

"Why would the FBI be after either of us? Makes no sense."

"Why would anyone be after either of us?" she asked in frustration.

Jake had no answer. But clearly she'd started him thinking along other lines. "I have a friend in the FBI." Jake dialed his car's speakerphone so Cassidy could hear. "Special Agent Fields, please."

It took only a moment for the line to ring through. "Fields speaking."

"Hi, Sam, it's Jake."

"Where are you? No, don't tell me. I don't want to know. I talked to Harrison last night."

Jake's employee had been busy.

"He woke me up and asked me to do some checking. Those names came up clean."

So Jake had been right. The possible FBI identification their pursuers had flashed at the clerk in the print shop had to be fake—just using it was a felony. But whoever was after them obviously wasn't worried about the law.

"Could the investigation be buried deeper than the usual files?"

"Unlikely. Whatever kind of trouble you're in, Jake, it's organized."

"Tell me something I don't know."

"The cops found no prints or fibers or DNA at Atkins's house that didn't belong there. Of course, forensics isn't done with the evidence yet. But the place is clean. Too clean, if you get my drift."

"You mean someone came back and wiped it?"

"Looks like."

Jake hung up the phone and Cassidy gave him time to digest the current turn of events. The average citizen would have been caught by their pursuers long ago. Without Jake's contacts, knowledge and resources, she would never have escaped.

Uneasily she looked out the side mirror at the traffic behind them. Nothing seemed out of the ordinary. Spanish moss draped towering oak trees that shaded parts of the two-lane road. Farm trucks pulled over as a fire truck whizzed past, siren blaring. Jake pulled over, too.

In the far distance, ahead of them, she saw either rain clouds or smoke. Considering the fire truck's speed, she figured lightning or a stray cigarette butt had started another fire. With the drought worsening, many acres had been lost. Cassidy had seen television news of homes, even entire towns enveloped by uncontrollable flames.

Jake pulled back onto the highway, and behind them Cassidy saw other cars do the same. But one particular vehicle made her forehead break out in a sweat. The vehicle wasn't flowing in the normal traffic pattern. It passed two and three cars at once, swerving back and forth dangerously.

"Jake! Behind us."

JAKE TOOK ONE LOOK in the rearview mirror, watched the car swerve in and out of traffic with precision and stepped on the gas. Whoever was sitting behind the wheel of that car knew his business, and although Jake had a head start, the SUV couldn't match the other vehicle's maneuverability on the road.

When Jake couldn't pass safely on the left, he used the shoulder to pass illegally on the right. A cop car and a speeding ticket would be welcome right now.

Up ahead the traffic wound through the rolling hills like a lazy snake. A smoky haze impaired his vision.

Jake reached into the standard-equipment satchel Harrison had left him behind the front seat, pulled out a pair of binoculars and handed them to Cassidy. "We may have to go off-road to lose them."

"But, Jake, there's a fire up ahead. We could be driving right into it if we leave the road."

Although she protested, she focused the binoculars. Jake's illegal use of the shoulder earned him angry glares from other drivers, honking horns and the occasional finger. He didn't blame them, but he didn't react to their frustration. He had his hands full staying ahead of the chase car, which was gaining on them by the minute.

"Cassidy, find me a dirt road, a bike path, a deer trail."

"I'm looking."

He bit his tongue to refrain from telling her to look harder. Cassidy was doing as he asked, and he knew she had to be frightened. Although keeping her alive was more important than worrying about what she might think of him, he still took care not to push her too hard. So far, he'd managed to keep the veneer of civilized polish he'd fought so hard to acquire. Not only didn't he want Cassidy to see him lose his cool, he wasn't sure if she'd continue to cooperate if she saw how he fought when he was fighting for his life. Jake knew all the dirty tricks. He'd used them to survive and if necessary, he'd use them to protect Cassidy, but he'd prefer to avoid situations where he would have to.

"See anything yet?"

"Maybe. We need to get closer."

"I'm trying."

The highway's shoulder vanished and forced Jake to drive on the grass. With the way the SUV bumped and swayed, and with the smoke thickening up ahead, he didn't know how Cassidy could focus through the binoculars.

"I see something. Maybe. Can you cut across the road?" she asked.

With bumper-to-bumper traffic slowed to less than five miles an hour, there was no room to cross the highway. Jake simply held his hand on the horn and prayed someone would move out of the way. Luckily several drivers complied, leaving him room to maneuver.

Jake drove as quickly as he dared. While SUVs were comfortable vehicles, they tended to be top-heavy and overturned more easily than a low-slung car. Hurrying wouldn't do them any good if he rolled into a ditch. But he longed to hide somewhere before their pursuers could see where they'd gone.

"There!" Cassidy pointed to a fenced pasture.

Along the fence, a dirt road beckoned. Without hesitation, Jake skidded onto the road. Dust flew up, marking the spot where they'd turned. Jake hoped the trail he'd left would be obscured by the smoke.

Cassidy flicked on the radio, searching for a Tampa station. "Maybe we can find out about the fire."

But she couldn't find any news stations with up-to-the-minute information about the fire. They were on their own. And if he wasn't mistaken, the smoke had thickened. The dirt road was narrowing, and tree branches scraped the vehicle's sides. Jake pressed on.

While the smoke provided excellent cover from their pursuers, it could also mean they were driving straight into a forest fire.

"The smoke's worse." Cassidy gave up on the radio and adjusted the air-conditioning fan. "Maybe we should turn around."

"I'm hoping this dirt road leads to a crossroad." They hit a bump. "Maybe something with pavement."

"Do I get a vote?" Cassidy braced her hands on the dash. "I'd rather face a bullet than burn to death."

Jake heard the fear in her voice and couldn't blame her. Yet he knew their pursuer was behind them. He'd rather take his chances with the unknown in front of him. Still, he tried to reassure Cassidy. "People don't usually die from the actual fire but from smoke inhalation."

"Great. I feel ever so much better now."

Jake reached over, took her hand and gave it a reassuring squeeze. He refused to lie and tell her they'd be fine when he had no idea if that was true. Cassidy squeezed his hand back, and then, as if realizing that he needed it to drive, she let go.

She raised the binoculars to her eyes. "There's a road up ahead." Her voice rose with hope and excitement, then leveled with disappointment. "But it's not paved. Still dirt."

Jake reached the intersection to find no more than another dirt path through the woods. Now they had a choice to make. They'd been traveling north. Should they head west, back toward Brooksville and the way they'd come? Or should they head east, toward their destination, Gainesville, and hope they'd somehow bypassed the worst of the fire?

As much as Jake hated to stop, he needed to make an intelligent informed decision. He needed to consult his map. But since he didn't know exactly where he'd left the highway or how far they'd driven in a straight line since then, he had to guess at their location.

Suddenly an idea struck him, and he smacked his forehead at his stupidity. He'd forgotten that part of the gear Harrison packed was a global-positioning-satellite system. They'd recently added the device to their standard equipment, and Jake had plain forgotten about it. Mistakes like that could get them killed.

But he wasn't about to waste time blaming himself for the error. Not now, anyway. "Damn it. I forgot about the GPS."

"The what?"

"It's a positioning instrument."

Cassidy frowned. "You have a navigational system in the SUV?"

"A portable unit." He pulled out the device, hit a button, and a satellite automatically fed him their longitude and latitude and then plotted his location on a map. Although the smoke was thick enough to restrict their vision to a hundred yards, Jake now knew exactly where he was. He pointed to the blinking dot on the screen. "This is where we are."

"So we aren't lost?" Cassidy still sounded skeptical, and he couldn't blame her.

He'd pinpointed their exact location and where they needed to go. But he still didn't know if any roads connected the two spots.

"We aren't much better off than we were before,

are we." Although Cassidy clearly tried to hide the discouragement in her voice, he heard it. "We still can't pinpoint the fire's location relative to where we are now."

"Yes, we can!"

Again he reached into his equipment bag. "These are infrared goggles. Heat sensitive. We use them to determine if someone's inside a building." Jake slipped the goggles over his eyes. The world suddenly changed from greens and grays to reds and browns. Red indicated heat.

Cassidy coughed in the worsening smoke. "Can you see anything?"

The goggles hadn't been designed for the purpose for which he was using them, but they worked quite well all the same. "The fire is west of here. Since we left the highway, we bypassed the worst of it." Jake removed the goggles and grinned. "I think we've lost them, Sunshine. I've seen no trace of a car sending dust into the air behind."

"Really?"

"We're safe now. We can just head on up to the University of Florida."

It took another hour of patient driving and a few U-turns, but Jake finally found a small paved road that led to a two-lane road that deposited them on a highway. At noon, only a few hours behind schedule, they stopped for gas and lunch.

Jake tried to check in with Harrison after their meal. When he said hello and Harrison told him he had the wrong number, Jake knew the line was bugged again.

With a frown, he turned off the phone's power.

He'd stop at a pay phone and keep his call under sixty seconds so it couldn't be traced.

"How did they bug the line so fast?" Cassidy asked, figuring out what had happened.

"Usually someone puts a device in the phone line or in the receiver. But Harrison's too smart to let that happen. We have detection equipment at the office."

"So how's it being done?"

"Through satellite transmission or at the phone company itself."

With a sinking feeling, Jake wondered once again exactly who he was up against. This foe had resources way beyond the normal criminal's means. Jake had heard rumors the government could listen to any phone call through the new digital technology. If the government could tap in, maybe others could, too. But who?

Eventually Jake found a pay phone. Harrison answered on the first ring. "The bodyguard you hired can't find your younger sister, and the other guard hasn't checked in."

"Keep trying. Anything else?"

"Don't come back here. There's heat everywhere."

"Heat" meant that whoever was after him was checking with his neighbors, friends and co-workers. They would keep watching his house and Cassidy's, their places of work, their regular haunts.

"Any idea what's going on?" Jake asked with mounting frustration.

"I was hoping you could tell me."

On that unsatisfactory note, the conversation ended. Jake and Cassidy finished their drive to the university, but Jake took no chances. After exiting the highway, he ducked into the first car wash he could find. He gave the vehicle a thorough washing, including the interior, so that no dirt, mud or foliage could identify the area where the car had been driven. He dropped Cassidy off at a corner store before going to a used-car lot where he swapped the SUV, trading down and leaving a fake name that matched the SUV's title.

While at the store, Cassidy shopped with cash, buying them hats, sunglasses and even a few wigs to use as disguises. Jake transferred their belongings to the old model BMW that he had bought, careful to leave nothing behind. Jake wanted an inconspicuous car that had some power. He knew Cassidy felt safer with his deception, but his ruse would only take them so far. Whoever was after him had technology and resources that were far above the ordinary.

If Jake hadn't known better, he might have thought he was dealing with a government operation. But if the feds wanted him, the cops would have put out an all-points bulletin for his arrest. And that hadn't happened. Not back at the restaurant where he and Cassidy had eaten dinner and all this chasing business had started. Later, Detective Fields would have told him if the cops were after him.

Luckily Jake wasn't without resources of his own. He had plenty of cash, several fake IDs, even one for Cassidy in which he could insert her picture. But the IDs would only go so far.

The fake documents might get him onto an airplane and out of the country, but they were vulnerable to a background check or even a casual investigation. Their faked driver's licenses, no matter how carefully forged, wouldn't survive a check with the Division of Motor Vehicles, where there were no such persons on file.

However, Jake didn't count himself out. He had his own connections and his wits. And if all else failed, he had a Swiss bank account, lots of cash and passports so that they could leave the country. While those kinds of documents were unusual for most P.I.s, Jake specialized in missing persons, and he often had to search for them outside the U.S. So he was always prepared.

He hoped it wouldn't come to that. Jake had no intention of leaving his sisters—not before they'd even had a chance to meet.

He picked Cassidy up in the new vehicle and kept his contingency plans to himself. No need to worry Cassidy unnecessarily. No need to get closer to her than necessary. The only good part about the pursuit today had been that he had been too busy to dwell on their kiss last night. Good Lord, the woman could kiss! He'd closed that off, done a good job of pretending it had never happened. But in quiet moments the kiss came back to haunt him.

For his peace of mind, he wished he could leave her behind, somewhere safe. But where? Hiding became difficult, almost impossible, when he didn't know who was after them. They had to keep going, figure out the puzzle before their pursuers caught up with them.

If Jake hadn't had Cassidy with him, he would have considered setting a trap and letting whoever was after him walk into it. A risky move, but one that could yield results. But he didn't dare take that chance with

Cassidy's life. Although she was holding up well, he wouldn't place her in that kind of danger—not while he had a choice.

Running while they searched for clues was still their best option. So he would keep Cassidy with him. Twenty-four/seven. Although he dreaded the evening hours when they were alone and his thoughts turned from business to personal matters, no way could he leave her unprotected. Right now, wherever he went, she went. Wherever they finally slept tonight, they would be together. And she'd want answers to the questions he'd seen in her eyes. Questions about why he'd pushed her away from that kiss. Questions about his feelings. Questions about his thoughts.

Only, he didn't have any answers.

Chapter Seven

Cassidy tugged on the curly auburn wig with the fly-away bangs that hid her blond hair. The damn thing itched in the heat, and she hoped the makeup that changed her complexion didn't run and expose her real skin tone. She glanced at Jake and refrained from chuckling. The dark-haired, light-eyed and olive-skinned detective had been transformed into someone she never would have recognized, thanks to a makeup kit he kept for disguises in the same bag as his electronic gear. Nonprescription contact lenses made his eyes a deep-sea green. Dark facial makeup made him look Hispanic, and a rakish mustache and hat completed his disguise.

But when he spoke with a Spanish accent to the secretary at the university's admissions office, Cassidy had to keep her lower jaw from dropping. Jake had missed his calling. He could have been an actor. He'd even changed his walk, strutting, rather than gliding.

The smile he gave the woman was pure charm. "I need to look up a student's records from over thirty years ago, ma'am."

"Thirty years ago?"

"*Sí.* My parents went to university here."

The secretary shook her head. "Our computer records don't go back that far." She pushed a form toward Jake. "If you fill this request out, someone might get back to you, but don't hold your breath."

Jake ignored the form. "I was told it would be easier to apply for medical school if I could prove my parents attended the university."

"That's true." The secretary smiled at Jake and fluffed her hair. "Why don't you try the library?" Her smile suggested she'd like to get to know Jake better.

"The library?" Jake asked.

"Yes. The student yearbooks might be a good starting point."

Cassidy and Jake walked across the pleasant campus as chattering students strolled and biked by. One student played Frisbee with his dog, some flew elaborate kites, and others pretended to study as they checked out the opposite sex.

The cool air of the library was a welcome relief after the midday heat. It didn't take long to find the yearbook section. While Jake scanned the records, Cassidy did a little research of her own.

They needed to find someone who remembered Jake's parents. Someone who could tell them if his parents had changed their names and why. Cassidy started with a list of professors, but found few teachers who had been at the university that long. She thought it highly unlikely that any of those professors would recall a student from so long ago, but considered the effort worth a try if they didn't find anything else.

Next she tried old newspapers on microfiche. She searched under his parents' names and the fake names, but found nothing. Cassidy still wasn't about to give up. She'd check the records of every fraternity house on campus if she had to.

When she tried the name on the university diploma and found that Michael Scott had belonged to Pi Epsilon Lamda, excitement raced through her. Fraternities often kept track of their members, hitting them up for donations, arranging reunions. Maybe they'd have a record of Jake's father's address or some pictures.

Cassidy copied the information and hurried to Jake to show him what she'd found. A coed had taken the chair next to Jake and was helping him search the library material. While the pesky blonde sat close to him, Jake only had eyes for the information in the book before him.

When Cassidy appeared, the coed gave her the once-over, shrugged as if to say Jake could do better, then removed herself from the chair. "He's all yours, honey. He's got 'taken' written all over him."

Uncomfortable with the girl's remark, Cassidy moved the chair farther away from Jake before taking it. If Jake had heard the girl, he didn't indicate it by so much of a flicker of an eyelash. His thoughts seemed far away, as if he was thinking about the past. Cassidy didn't know whether to be flattered that he wasn't interested in another woman or insulted that he didn't appear to notice when she took the coed's chair.

She wondered if Jake had never fallen in love due to lack of time. Of course, she didn't know that he hadn't fallen in love. But he'd never married. Maybe he couldn't commit to a woman when the past and finding his sisters placed such a strain on his time. Whatever the reason, she was glad they had this opportunity to get to know one another again. She only wished the circumstances could have been more normal.

"What did you find?" she asked, keeping her news to herself for the moment.

"I found a picture of Mary Lou Ellis." He pointed at a picture in the yearbook, then held up the picture of the woman she'd thought might have been his mother from the photo that she'd found in her father's attic.

She used a pencil to scratch her scalp under the itchy wig. "They're the same woman. Your mother did change her name."

"Not necessarily." Jake twisted his mustache. "We simply now know that the woman in both pictures went by the name of Mary Lou Ellis. We still don't know if she's my mother. And since I can't recall my mother's maiden name—"

"Not many five-year-old boys would."

"—we may never know if Mary Lou is the same woman as Janet."

Cassidy peered at the picture, sure she saw a resemblance between the woman and Jake. "Who's the other woman? The one standing next to Mary Lou?"

He read the name under the picture. "Donna Rodale. Why?"

Something in the black-and-white photograph suggested a friendship between the two students. Maybe it was the expression in the eyes or the relaxed smiles, as if they'd been sharing a secret when the photograph was snapped. "I think we should look her up and see if she remembers Mary Lou Ellis."

"Good idea." Jake copied the picture and information. "Harrison can track her down."

"Even if she's married and changed her name?"

"Social-security numbers don't change when you marry."

Cassidy watched Jake close the old yearbook with reluctance. Clearly he wasn't satisfied, and she hoped to perk him up. "I may have found something else."

Jake leaned back in his chair and tugged on his mustache, his eyes glittering with mischief. "I knew I'd kept you around for a reason."

She warmed inside when Jake teased her and was all the happier to have made herself useful. "Michael Scott belonged to a fraternity."

"And?" Jake didn't seem overly excited.

"They keep records."

"They do?"

"They send the names to national registries."

"So?" Jake folded his arms over his chest.

She wanted to shake him out of his complacency. But then she recalled that Jake hadn't had the opportunity to attend college. He wasn't familiar with why her find could be important. "The chapter house may have a record of a previous residence or where Michael Scott moved after he left college. If we get lucky, we might find someone who lived there at the same time who remembers him. Trust me, those fraternity guys are like army buddies. They're close."

Impulsively she grabbed Jake's hands, pulled him to his feet and twirled him around in an excited dance. "They drink together and party together and—"

Jake shot her a wide grin of approval under his black mustache. "Okay, okay. Lead on, Sherlock. Take me to the frat house."

His arms around her felt good, and she was really pleased with herself for bringing that grin to his face. "Don't let them hear you say that."

"What?"

"'Frat house' is considered an insult. It's a chapter house or the PEL house."

"Got it."

BUT HE DIDN'T GET IT. Why did people join fraternities? Jake wondered. Maybe because he'd grown up in an assortment of homes with different kinds of people, he found variety fascinating. He didn't like the idea of limiting himself to people who thought like he did. He supposed a shrink might say that was because he didn't like himself. He preferred to believe he was broad-minded.

They found Pi Epsilon Lamda on a street with other houses. Although each flew its own emblem, the houses differed in looks—some were A-frames, some Colonials, some contemporary. Most were brick with large eaves, rich landscapes and yards that needed watering.

Cassidy might never have been on this campus, but she appeared right at home. She smiled at a jock in a sleeveless T-shirt decorated with orange alligators biting one another's tails; he was petting his dog. She seemed comfortable, friendly and at ease with her world. One of the reasons Jake enjoyed being with Cassidy was her self-confidence. She didn't hold back, enjoying each moment without worrying about consequences. Open to a variety of people and circumstances, she met the world with a sense of optimism that cracked through Jake's cynicism.

Just being around Cassidy made him more open to new feelings. Food tasted better. Smells were sharper. And beating the danger that followed them seemed possible.

After years of schooling himself to turn a stoic face to the world, Jake could feel himself opening up again. And whenever Cassidy noticed his voice betraying his emotions, she further shattered his protective shell. Oddly enough, he didn't mind. There was a freedom in letting himself feel, but a danger, as well.

Jake still maintained control of his actions. He recognized that he possessed special feelings concerning Cassidy, ones she might never return. Had she ever had those feelings for him? He suspected she still considered him a friend, just as she always had. That she wanted a sexual fling didn't necessary indicate any deeper emotions. Her impulsive nature made reading her difficult. But either way he could deal with it. He had to.

The fraternity jock stopped petting his dog, wiped his hand on his T-shirt, then offered his hand to Cassidy. "Can I help you?"

Jake didn't like the way the kid eyed Cassidy, as if she was some simpering coed impressed by muscles. What bothered Jake even more was that he'd noticed. He hadn't been with Cassidy for forty-eight hours and already he was seeing things he'd never before observed. But he wasn't losing control. Being perceptive about strangers wasn't a weakness. Not when danger could come from any direction.

Cassidy's grin widened. "Would you be a Pi Epsilon Lamda?"

The kid nodded with pride. "Sure am."

Jake smoothly inserted himself into the conversation. "My dad belonged."

"Cool." The kid's smile widened.

Cassidy took Jake's hand and explained the reason for their visit. "Jake's dad said if he ever came by this way to look him up on the composite."

Jake didn't like her using his real name, but he couldn't fault her. He had neglected to tell her otherwise. Damn it. What else had he forgotten? Maybe he wasn't in as much control as he'd thought. Opening himself up to new feelings had a definite downside. But keeping his mind on his work, and only his work, seemed so limiting, especially when he'd glimpsed the possibility of more.

The jock led them inside and waved them over to a wall filled with framed pictures. Each giant frame was composed of members' head shots and dated with the academic school year. Since the pictures were placed in consecutive order on the wall, Cassidy easily zoomed in on the one photo of Michael Scott.

"That's him." She checked the composites for the year before and the year after. "He only joined up for one year. I bet that's unusual." While Jake wrote the list of names on a pad, she turned back to the Pi Epsilon Lamda man. "Would you have records of who Mr. Scott might have roomed with? I can't recall the man's name, but Jake's dad wanted us to look him up.''

''You might ask the caretaker,'' the jock offered. ''He lives in the attic and he's been here since the Second World War. Go up four flights and knock.''

Cassidy strode through the fraternity house with the boldness of a member. Half-dressed jocks, loud music and messy rooms didn't even slow her down. Jake wondered if she'd spent time during college in houses like this one, then shoved the thought from his mind. He didn't want to think about Cassidy partying with other men.

Instead, he leaned forward and whispered in her ear. ''Try not to use my real name, Sunshine.''

She turned on the second-story staircase landing to face him, her smile fading. ''Oh, I'm so sorry. I wasn't thinking.'' She glanced toward the front entrance, the way they'd come in, as if expecting their pursuer to arrive and capitalize on her error at any moment. ''Is someone tailing us again?''

''I haven't seen anyone. But it's better to play it safe and not leave any clues.'' He could see the worry in her eyes and sought to bring back her smile. ''Hey, it probably doesn't matter. If anyone comes here and asks questions about visitors, they'll know it was us.''

''Even with our disguises?''

''How many people do you think ask about thirty-year-old pictures?'' he asked wryly.

''You've got a point.'' A teasing light brightened her eyes. ''A very good point...Norbert.''

''That's not the most flattering name I can think of,'' he complained, but enjoyed watching her eyes brighten again. He enjoyed her banter as much as he enjoyed her sharp mind and as much as he'd enjoyed that sizzling kiss, the one he wasn't going to think about.

"What would you prefer I call you?" She didn't wait for him to answer, simply threaded her arm through his and accompanied him up the stairs. "I've always thought pet names are interesting. I have a friend, Lisa, who lives in New Jersey. Her husband Dave calls her 'babe.' She calls him 'stupid.'"

He could tell from her tone that she was pushing him, trying to get a rise out of him, but he refused to let her chatter distract him. He'd already noted a back staircase they could use for escape if someone suddenly burst through the front door. If necessary, they could go out the window onto the roof and flee toward the next block. But he'd hate to leave his pack behind. He would have carried it with him, but it looked like what it was—supplies for a man on a mission.

They stopped outside a thick attic door and knocked. Jake wasn't surprised when an elderly gentleman answered, a man old enough to have served in the Second World War. He moved with a spryness surprising for a man his age. Light-blue eyes sparkled with intelligence as he looked at Jake, then Cassidy, before sticking out his hand and introducing himself. "I'm Doc. Not an M.D. Not a Ph.D. I just fix whatever gets broke in this place."

Cassidy shook Doc's hand. "I'm Angela, but you can call me Angel." She grinned with devilment at Jake. "And this is Herman. We wanted to ask you about one of the men in a picture downstairs."

Jake expected Doc to go downstairs so they could show him the picture, but instead, he invited them into his room. The steep ceiling of the attic and the polished oak floors that gleamed with fresh wax were a perfect backdrop to the antiques scattered about.

"What was the man's name?"

"Michael Scott."

"I remember him."

Jake and Cassidy exchanged a skeptical glance. Doc must have caught it, because he chuckled. "Class of sixty-nine. Dark hair, big shoulders. He joined us his junior year."

"Would you happen to recall anything else about him?" Jake asked, amazed at the old man's memory.

Pale-blue eyes gave him a hard look. "Such as?"

"Who he was friends with or who he might have roomed with?" Cassidy asked.

"His roomie was a fellah by the name of Boon Aldrich."

Jake took out a notebook and pen, started to write, but Doc shook his head. "He died in Vietnam."

"You have an amazing memory," Jake complimented the old man.

"It's not that amazing. Sure, I can remember what happened years ago like it was yesterday. Unfortunately I can't remember what I had for breakfast."

"Can you recall anyone else?"

Doc snapped his fingers. "Michael kept to himself. Didn't party much, but there was one fellah he was tight with. Went by the name of Blake Saunders. Heard he lives over in Jacksonville. You can look him up in the alumni section of the university's Web site."

"Thank you, Doc. You've been very helpful." Cassidy looked edgy as she watched a car pull down the street and park in front of the fraternity house. Two doors slammed and trees blocked their view of the newcomers.

Jake didn't think there was much chance Doc would recall anything else, but one more question was worth a shot, worth using a few precious extra seconds. "Do you recall if Michael Scott had a girlfriend?"

"He sure did. A pretty little girl with a mind as sharp as a tack. Her name was one of those Southern double things. Mary Jo. Mary Ann. Mary Lou. Yes, it was Mary Lou. Sorry, I can't recall her last name. Michael always said he was going to marry that girl."

Jake heard a commotion downstairs. Quickly he said thanks, and he and Cassidy turned and left.

Hoping they weren't trapped, Jake hurried Cassidy down to the second floor before taking the back staircase. He couldn't quite hear over the loud music what the yelling downstairs was about.

Jake preferred not to be seen, not to have a confrontation here. Although they wore disguises, they wouldn't pass a close inspection. If they could sneak out the rear and circle back to their car without being seen, he would consider himself very fortunate.

The back stairs led down to an empty kitchen. As they hurried through, Jake wondered how their pursuer could have found them so quickly. He hadn't made any phone calls or used a credit card. They'd switched vehicles and wore disguises. He could think of only a few ways someone could have caught up with them.

As they sprinted around the backyard toward the front, Cassidy whispered. "How did they find us?"

It was amazing how sometimes their minds worked on the same puzzles. Jake opened a gate and peered down the street. He didn't see anyone, but he could still hear the argument inside. "Either they're psychic—"

"I don't believe in that stuff."

"—or they planted a bug on something we own."

Cassidy frowned but didn't slow her footsteps. "But when? How? We switched cars and phones, and no one's been close enough to touch us since that man came to my house."

"Or they knew we would come here." Jake parted branches and helped Cassidy through a hedge. "Just be glad they followed us, instead of waiting in the car."

Cassidy let out a long sigh. "How could anyone predict our movements? We didn't even know we were coming here until we accessed the computer in the library."

"Bingo!" Jake snapped his fingers as he and Cassidy hurried to the car. "There must be some kind of code attached to the Web site. Any inquiries about my father's name triggers an investigation."

"Triggers an investigation just like my phone call did?"

"Exactly. The only reason someone targeted you was because you showed interest in my parents' past."

Cassidy snapped her seat belt into place just as two men exited the fraternity. "Drive, Jake. Get us out of here."

"I'm on it." Jake burned rubber as he peeled out

of the parking space and down the street. "Pull out the map."

Cassidy did as he asked. "And head where?"

"Find the biggest intersection of highways in town and give me directions to it."

Cassidy sighed. "You don't know where we're going, do you?"

"Of course I do." Jake steered a hard right. "Away from here."

Cassidy peered over her shoulder at the other car. "How do they keep finding us?"

"We're leaving a trail and they're good." Jake caught a yellow light and stepped on the gas, clearing the intersection just as the light turned red.

"You mean you know how they're following us?" Cassidy demanded.

"We're leaving clues, Sunshine. The only way to avoid leaving any clues is to hole up and keep our heads down. But if we do that, we'll never figure out who's after us." Jake merged into a stream of traffic. "We'll just have to stay one step ahead of them."

"How?"

"We'll try to be as unpredictable as possible."

Cassidy yanked the wig off her head and studied the map. "Hang your first left and then a right."

Jake checked the gas gauge and saw that they had only a quarter of a tank. He figured he had to lose their tail within the next half hour. His job would have been easier in a major city, at night or in a major thunderstorm. But the traffic remained light, the sun wouldn't set for several hours, and there wasn't a cloud in sight.

Sometimes a man had to make his own luck. Jake

saw the other car speed right through a red light. Two cars avoided a head-on collision, but crashed into vacant parked cars along the curb. Unfortunately the car chasing them kept right on coming.

"We're holding our own," Cassidy told him.

"We need to lose them before we hit the interstate. And I can't do that unless we widen our lead. Hold on."

Jake swung a hard right, then two quick lefts. Several cars honked, but at least he didn't cause any accidents. Beside him Cassidy stiffened. He caught sight of her pale face, her eyes wide with fear, but she didn't say a word in protest.

Instead, she pointed. "There, Jake. We can pull into that empty car wash and hide."

Jake checked the rearview mirror and realized he'd gained enough distance on the chase car to follow Cassidy's instructions. He veered into the self-serve car wash.

Beside him Cassidy tensed. He had to remind himself to breathe. Sixty seconds later the chase car barreled down the street. Jake kept his vehicle in gear, ready to speed off if they were spotted. But the other car sped by.

"How long until they figure out what happened?" Cassidy asked.

"A minute or two if we're lucky." Jake pulled a U-turn and headed back the way they'd come, wanting to put as many miles as possible between them and Gainesville.

He pulled onto the highway and headed north. At the same time, he took out his cell phone. He had to risk another phone call to Harrison. He dialed the number, hoping he wouldn't have to stop at a pay phone. By now, Harrison should have the encryption working so, even if the phone was still tapped, the conversation would sound like gibberish to outsiders.

"Are we clear?" he asked without any preliminary conversation.

"Keep it short," Harrison told him.

"Cassidy's going to read you a list of names. I want you to find out where these alumni currently live. The University of Florida has them registered."

"Gotcha."

"And Harrison?"

"Yeah, boss?"

"Don't leave any tracks."

Chapter Eight

Jake didn't want to drive too far in the wrong direction. Unfortunately, until Harrison got back to him, he had no idea where they would head next. He stopped for gas and asked if there were any local folks who ran a bed-and-breakfast and could put them up for the night.

The area didn't have many hotels, and Jake feared it would be too easy for their pursuers to find them if they checked into any national chain—all had computerized registries that could be hacked. When the gas-station attendant didn't make any suggestions, Jake returned to the car. He considered driving through the night, heading straight north to Georgia. But he hadn't slept much the night before, and tired people made mistakes.

"You ever heard of Blue Spring State Park?" he asked Cassidy.

She looked at him warily, her nose scrunched with distaste. While she enjoyed the outdoors, she preferred the creature comforts of luxury hotels to camping with mosquitoes. "I haven't slept in a tent since I was a kid."

"You didn't have a good time?" he asked, more to take her mind off their pursuers than to hear her version of the story again. He'd heard it before, a long time ago, and was surprised how clearly the details had stayed in his mind and how little the words had changed.

"Dad took me camping and a raccoon sneaked inside our tent. The animal uncapped our toothpaste and squirted it everywhere. He ate my candy bar, too."

She sounded just as indignant about that stolen candy bar as she had a decade ago. "You aren't supposed to keep food in your tent."

Suspicious, she peered into the back seat. "You don't have a tent in the trunk, do you?"

He shook his head. "As I recall, Blue Springs has cabins. It's off the St. John's River and shouldn't be crowded at this time of year. Plus, it's out-of-the-way. I don't think anyone will come looking for us there."

Cassidy folded up the map. "Cabins with beds, clean sheets and a hot shower?"

"Yeah. But I don't think they have a restaurant. So we'd better buy some food on the way."

Jake took a roundabout route, making sure he hadn't picked up a tail before stopping at a grocery store. While Cassidy shopped, Jake made an overnight reservation at the state park. Half an hour later they were back in the car.

The earlier tensions of the day slowly diminished, chased away by the bright Florida sunshine. As they turned off the highway onto a series of two-lane roads, it was almost as if they were traveling back in time and leaving their present-day problems far behind.

They pulled into the family campground after dusk. Jake registered for their cabin under an assumed name. They unloaded their supplies and belongings, working together easily, almost like an old married couple. He took the heavy bags inside, she stowed the supplies.

Their cabin sat on a small hill overlooking the natural spring that fed the river. The one-room interior, a combination of kitchen, living room and bedroom, might have been little more than functional, but it was clean and adequate for their needs. While Cassidy put away the food in the refrigerator, Jake lit the charcoal on a grill.

Breakfast and the hectic hours since seemed far away. Jake knew they would return to the dangerous outside world all too soon and was determined to appreciate this peaceful interlude.

Around him the sounds of children at play slowly wound down as mothers and fathers put the kids to bed. A light breeze chased away mosquitoes, leaving him to tend the grill while he listened to the pleasant chirp of crickets and the croaks of tree frogs.

Cassidy joined him on the porch, handing him two steaks, shrimp with barbecue sauce and corn on the cob that she'd slathered in butter and wrapped in aluminum foil. "Be right back."

He placed the steaks on the grill and set aside the shrimp and corn to cook later. Her face flushed, probably from heat, since the cabin lacked air-conditioning, Cassidy returned and handed him a glass of white wine with an ice cube. She'd changed into short shorts and a skimpy top, twisted her hair onto her head and placed her own glass against her forehead.

"Mmm. That feels so good." Cassidy swirled her chilled wine with a finger.

Jake suddenly had the urge to lick the wine from that finger, but he didn't act on the erotic thought, although his voice veered toward husky. "I hear you're supposed to drink it, not bathe in it."

As if by mutual agreement, they put aside the problems of the day. Cassidy plucked her finger from the wine and flicked a few drops in his direction. "In my younger days I might have tossed the glass at you and given you a shower, but now..."

"Now?"

"I'd hate to waste a good drink." She sank into a chair, raised her wineglass to him in a salute, then sipped, her lips soft and full against the glass, reminding him of when those lips had been pressed to his.

He shoved the image away, concentrating on her last words to him. Did she expect him to believe that she no longer allowed her playful impulses to dictate her actions? That she wouldn't douse him with the wine if he teased her? Even now, he could see the mischievous upturn of her lips, the sparkling flash of daring in her eyes and the challenging tilt of her chin.

What did she want from him? That Cassidy was ready to relax, he had no doubt. The sensuous way she tucked her toes under her tush and the indolent way she let her head rest on the lounge chair, wisps of curls escaping her magnificent golden hair, appealed to him in a place where rational thoughts couldn't quite overcome primitive needs.

His every instinct told him to pick her up, toss her over his shoulder and carry her into the bedroom. Take what her teasing offered.

Jake, instead, turned back to the steaks. Just because they weren't in immediate danger was no reason to let her sway him from his course of action. He might think he had himself under control; he believed he could handle the ramifications of his actions, but did he really want to put himself to the test?

Oblivious to his inner turmoil, Cassidy sipped her wine. "I hope you like onions and garlic."

He suspected he'd like anything she prepared. "You made a salad?"

"And there's watermelon for dessert. I'll bet I can still spit the seeds farther than you can."

He'd bet she could, too. Especially since his mouth went dry every time he looked at her. She wasn't a classic beauty with model thinness. Her face was round and healthy, glowing with vitality. Her eyes could be fierce when she concentrated on a problem, or they could go soft and misty when she relaxed, as she was doing now.

"Want to place a bet?" he asked, his gaze lingering speculatively on her face, letting her set the terms.

"Sure." Her face brightened with amusement. "If I win, I get to kiss you again."

Jake made his decision, determined he could handle the simmering tension, after all. He'd resisted her kisses before; he could do so again. And perhaps his kisses could persuade her to care about him more than she'd thought possible. "And if I win, we go for a midnight swim."

"I didn't bring a swimsuit." Cassidy grinned up at

him, neither particularly alarmed, nor the least bit intimidated by the idea.

"I didn't bring a suit, either."

"It's a family park."

Jake checked his watch. It was only nine-thirty. Several couples still strolled along the banks of the spring. One man fished, his line static in the water. Jake suspected that by midnight, they'd have the place to themselves.

"It doesn't matter," Cassidy teased him. "You're going to lose. We have a deal?"

"Deal." He felt more than satisfied with the arrangement. How could he not be? A steak dinner, with Cassidy to share it, followed by a moonlit walk. A watermelon-seed-spitting contest and either another of her wonderful kisses or a midnight swim. Jake could handle the evening and keep his emotions locked down tight while enjoying himself. What could good conversation and a few kisses hurt?

"Oh, Jake..."

"Hmm?"

"You didn't specify *where* I get to kiss you, so the choice is mine."

At her suggestive words, Jake's stomach knotted. How could he have forgotten what a giant tease she could be? However, he had no intention of letting her know how her suggestion could get to him. Instead, he simply handed her his empty wineglass. "The chef is thirsty. How about another drink, woman?"

"Sure." She rose to her feet with the ease of a dancer, leaned over to take his glass and peered at the steak. "I like my meat pink."

"Is that so?"

''Tender.''

She leaned a little closer. Jake refused to step back. He tried to say something but ended up just clearing his throat.

''And juicy.''

Cassidy must have seen the gleam of recklessness in Jake's eyes because she suddenly whirled, snatched the glass from his hand and escaped to the kitchen.

It took several minutes after Cassidy's departure before Jake's breathing returned to anything approaching normal. The woman certainly knew how to turn up the heat. But this was no longer the innocent teenage girl of his memories. Cassidy was all woman, capable of caring and friendship and even love. And he suspected she knew exactly how she was affecting him—physically.

He wanted to make love to her. What red-blooded American male wouldn't? She'd kindled the slow-burning embers into a white-hot flame.

But Jake was no longer a kid, either. And he had feelings for this woman, feelings that Cassidy knew nothing about.

To him, Cassidy Atkins had always been special. She had a warmth that drew him, an openness that never promised more than she was willing to deliver. And what she wanted was a night of passion where they could forget the danger closing in on them.

He didn't know if he could continue to resist her bold flirting. Didn't know if he could keep his physical needs on the back burner. Didn't know if he could deal with the emotions she'd stoked. Didn't dare let himself believe there could be more.

CASSIDY COULDN'T EAT another bite. Jake had cooked
the steaks to perfection, and the shrimp sauce had just
the right amount of sweet with the tart. She wished
she could say the same for Jake. Although he held up
his end of the conversation and his smiles seemed
genuine, he kept an air of reserve around him at all
times that left her wondering what was going through
his mind.

Maybe it was the danger, maybe it was running into
a wet and naked Jake as he'd stepped out of the
shower, or maybe it was sharing every minute of their
day, but Jake seemed to be growing more appealing
by the hour. And Cassidy longed to delve into her
emotions, open herself to the possibilities. But she
had to guard herself against her impulsive nature.
Maybe she should be cautious, play it safe. Then
again maybe her normal impulsiveness was her way
of avoiding dealing with consequences.

She'd tried to consider a relationship between them
with all the logic she could command. She liked Jake,
always had. He'd been a good friend to a teenage girl,
a better friend to the woman she'd become. Jake had
saved her life, and he might be the only person keeping her alive as he hid her from their pursuer.

Yet while she had no doubt he would risk his life
to save hers, he guarded his emotions as if they were
a treasure she might be out to steal. One minute he
seemed to trust her, sharing a glance or a touch, and
the next he withdrew into himself with an intensity
she found alarming.

She thought that if he didn't want to share his
thoughts, it meant he didn't have a high opinion of

her. And who wanted a man who didn't appreciate her?

You do.

Her conscience intruded and Cassidy didn't like it one bit, since it always seemed to happen when she was trying to fool herself.

So maybe I do want him, she admitted.

What are you going to do about it?

Well, kissing him didn't work. He'd had no trouble resisting the temptation to step things up to the next level.

Yes, he did. You heard his ragged breathing. Saw the gleam of passion. Heard the—

Okay. You made your point. Now go away and let me think.

Thinking isn't getting you anywhere.

I don't know what to do. He's holding back a part of himself I can't reach.

You aren't trying hard enough.

Easy for you to say. He's as stubborn as a mountain. I can't budge him.

Then make the mountain come to you.

How?

No answer. Where was her conscience when she needed it? Frustrated with her thoughts, she took their empty plastic dishes into the cabin and tossed them into the trash can. She rinsed her hands at the sink, turned around and almost bumped into Jake.

She took the paper towel he handed her and dried her hands. "Dinner was great, but I can't eat another bite."

Jake looked from the watermelon on the counter to Cassidy. "Going to welsh on our bet?"

"How about a walk? Maybe my stomach will make more room if we exercise."

"Sure."

Jake opened the door for her, and together they walked outside. She breathed in the warm night air, the earthy scent of cypress trees, springwater and grass. "It'll be good to stretch my legs."

"Hold on a second." Jake shook a can of mosquito repellent and sprayed some into his palm. "A former occupant left this and we should—"

"There's a breeze."

"Turn around, I'll do your shoulders."

That's not all he wants to do.

Hush. Let me enjoy.

Cassidy gave Jake her back and faced the deserted spring. Except for the night creatures, an owl, a few ducks and the frogs, they had the place to themselves.

His hand was warm, the bug spray cool. While his fingers on her neck and shoulders were no more personal than a masseur's, Cassidy enjoyed every efficient stroke. She was tempted to turn around and ask him to do her front. But then she recalled that the mountain had to come to her.

She took the can from Jake and sprayed some into her palm. The lemony scent was pleasant, and she decided there were other ways to play this game. "I'd better do my legs, too."

Cassidy found a log that a former camper had dragged over, probably to sit on and watch his family swim in the spring. She had a better use for the log. She propped one foot on it, then proceeded to spread the spray along her ankle, calf and thigh. She took her time, totally ignoring Jake, smoothing in the lotion and hoping he was wishing *his* hands were on her legs. Slowly, sensuously, she repeated the procedure on her other leg. Last, she dabbed more on her neck and upper chest.

Finally she turned to Jake. He wasn't even pretending not to watch. She stifled a grin, tugged his hand and made him sit on the log so she could reach his face. "Now, let me get your neck."

He wore full-length jeans and a short-sleeved shirt. She took her time, making sure she rubbed behind his ears, down his neck and forward to his throat and lower jaw. Jake sat still as stone until her palm caressed his cheek. Slowly he stood, took the can from her and set it on the log before wrapping an arm around her shoulders.

"There's a path along the spring that leads to the river."

Cassidy put her arm around his waist. His warmth and hardness and strength made her feel safe. Yet she didn't want to feel safe. She didn't want comfort. She wanted to push Jake into kissing her again, but she wasn't sure how. Somehow she had to break through the shell he'd built so carefully around himself. She wondered if he even knew it was there.

"Jake?"

"Mmm?"

Cassidy decided to take a chance. She knew she might inadvertently push him away, but ignoring whatever he was brooding over was no way to solve a problem. "Have you ever been in love?"

Jake's only answer was a shrug. Then he asked, "What about you?"

"I'm not closed to the possibility."

"You just haven't found the right guy?"

"It takes more than just the right guy. The timing has to be right."

"Sunshine, you're a real piece of work."

At his mocking endearment, she'd had enough. Without thinking, she planted her palms on Jake's chest and shoved. She took him by surprise, and he stumbled backward into the spring, landing on his backside with a loud splash.

She'd moved the mountain.

In the moonlight the astonished expression on his face was priceless. She'd treasure it forever. She started to laugh. And that was her mistake. In one second Jake's hand snaked out and pulled her into the spring with him.

She didn't care that she was now soaking wet. Tilting her head back, she looked at Jake. Although he was trying to keep a stern expression, she glimpsed amusement in his eyes.

His hands clasped her waist and he growled in her ear. "So you want to play rough, do you?"

His fingers found the ticklish spot between her ribs, and she splashed to get away. Jake blocked her way onto the bank, so she stood up, did a shallow racing dive and swam for the other side of the spring.

Jake caught her ankle before she'd made it ten feet. Breathless, she spun around and he dunked her. Cassidy went with his force, grasped his foot and yanked him down with her. They both surfaced, gasping for air.

While she treaded water, his taller height put him at an advantage. His feet still reached the bottom, and he reeled her in like a struggling mermaid. Cassidy threw her arms around his neck, and in a flash, Jake's demeanor changed from playful to serious. "Are you mad at me, Sunshine?"

Yes. "A little."

"Mind telling me why?" His voice was mild, almost deceptively so, for she heard the edge of steel underneath.

"You keep giving me mixed signals." She braced her hands on his shoulders and floated. "One moment you share your thoughts and feelings, and the next…you cut me out."

"I have my reasons."

"Ones you won't share." When he remained silent, she pulled back, floating free of him. "Tell me something, Jake. Who are you fighting here? Me? Or yourself?"

When he still remained silent, she sighed and took a stab at guessing his secret. "Whoever she was, she must have hurt you badly."

"What are you talking about?" he growled. "There is no other woman." He reached for her then and drew her gently back into his arms. "There's only been you, Sunshine."

"Me?" She wished the moon hadn't just hidden behind a cloud. She wanted to see his face better. "We were never… We were just…friends."

"That was all you wanted to believe," he told her softly.

And suddenly it hit her.

Jake had wanted more than she'd known.

Jake hadn't considered her just a friend.

Shock made her heart race. Jake must have loved

her. A long time ago he must have loved her, or he wouldn't still be wounded.

She had been the woman who'd hurt him because she'd never given him anything but her friendship. She winced as memories flooded back. She hadn't even been a very good friend. After she'd left for college and law school, she'd been so busy she'd let contact with him lapse. During summer vacations, she'd clerked for lawyers out west. On the rare occasions she'd come home, her father had always planned special trips for the two of them.

And Jake...she'd left him behind.

If Jake had grown up in a regular family with loving parents and siblings, her leaving might not have hurt him. But even back then, she might not have consciously thought about their friendship or analyzed it, but she'd known Jake's intensity, the way he felt about her. While she'd had other friends and dated other boys, to Jake, their relationship had been anything but casual.

And maybe that was why she'd heeded her own dream and headed to college. Jake's intensity had scared her. It scared her still. He hadn't been the kind of kid to steal a few kisses and see where they led.

Jake always had a plan for the future. Spontaneity wasn't in his vocabulary. She supposed he'd been forced to live that way to survive.

"I'm sorry, Jake."

"For what?"

"Not being a good enough friend. Not being what you wanted."

"Oh, I wanted you, Sunshine."

She noticed they were talking in the past tense.

Why didn't she want to think about the future? Because it scared her. Did she live for the moment because her mother had died before any of her goals had been fulfilled? Cassidy wondered when she would grow past the fear and think about tomorrow.

She really wasn't sure what Jake thought about her now. When he kissed her, the attraction between them sizzled. But that was lust. She knew instinctively that Jake didn't just want to make love. He wanted her to love him.

Maybe she'd been wise to leave without looking back ten years ago. Maybe that was what she should do now. Swim away. Go home.

Could she go home now? She didn't think of Jake as just a friend anymore. Did she want to keep enjoying life in a string of moments, or did she want to take a chance and look to tomorrow for love? As she looked at Jake, saw the intensity in his eyes, the determination in the set of his jaw, confusion almost overwhelmed her. She honestly didn't know what she wanted. But she did know she couldn't go home.

Someone would be waiting for her there. Someone who might very well kill her.

Chapter Nine

Jake damned himself for telling Cassidy the truth. He should have kept his mouth shut. But she had him feeling things that confused him. How could he think when she floated into his arms and looked at him with those earnest eyes?

When her teeth started to chatter, he began swimming. "Race you to the other side."

He swam, staying beside her, his thoughts churning harder than his arms. Cassidy was a strong swimmer, but he wasn't about to leave her behind in the dark.

He figured he'd frightened her away from any further intimacies for the night. But he should have known better. While the race across the spring had just given his swirling thoughts more time to spin, Cassidy seemingly had no such difficulties.

She waited for him to stand, then planted her palms on his chest as she had before. "I want to kiss you again."

He held perfectly still. "I didn't scare you off?"

"If that's what you intended, you failed. I can't make any promises. But I want…"

"What?"

"I don't know." She tossed her wet hair from her face. "I want us to take a chance. To see where we can go. Together."

She wanted him to trust her, and he didn't know if he could. She wanted them to go forward, without planning, without a safety net, without hesitation.

He was sure Cassidy hadn't considered the future. And when they finally went their own ways, there would be consequences to their actions.

She had more courage than he, a willingness to just accept the present without worrying about the future. But he wasn't made that way. He should just turn away, take the safer path. But in the moonlight, her lips glistened with promise, irresistibly drawing his head downward.

Somehow she had overcome his resistance to her, enabling him to kiss her with a freedom he'd never before known. It felt so good to let down his guard, not to think or plan or worry, to just feel. Feel her gossamer lips respond to his, feel her arms wind around his neck, her fingers intertwine in his hair, pulling him close.

She let out a tiny moan of desire, and the sound arrowed straight to his core, making him burn. Cassidy's kiss was like a magical potion that freed him from his past, made the future hazy and the present wonderful. He couldn't get enough of her.

Jake pressed her to him, letting her feel his hardness, letting her know how much he wanted her. He'd been so sure he could keep his feelings under control, but now he didn't know if he'd succeed. Cassidy had a way of overwhelming his nervous system. He couldn't copy the out-of-control, let's-do-what-we-want-and-damn-the-consequences perspective that other men seemed to adopt so easily.

He didn't want to make love to her and then miss her so badly that he'd be haunted by memories of this night for the rest of his life. Better not to know how good it could be. Better not to fall for her again. He had to back out while he still could.

Summoning up the inner strength to push away what he wanted most, he broke free of her embrace.

"Jake?" she whispered huskily.

He uttered the first excuse that came to mind. "I don't want you to catch cold."

"Cold?" She spit the word at him as if he'd uttered the worst of insults. "The only thing cold around here is you."

Jake let her swim away from him and watched her walk to the cabin. Talking only made things worse. But then, so did kissing her. He'd almost peeled off her wet clothes and made love to her right in the spring.

He had to be an idiot to refuse what she'd offered, but he couldn't bear to take her and then lose her again. Being with her twenty-four hours a day, sleeping under the same roof at night, was wearing down his resistance.

To work off the sexual energy, Jake swam laps back and forth across the spring. He gave Cassidy time to shower, go to bed and fall asleep before he finally exited the water. Stiff, bone weary, emotionally spent, he walked to the dark cabin.

Cassidy hadn't even left the porch light on.

He supposed he deserved her anger. He had no

business kissing her, then pulling back. Yet he couldn't seem to help himself.

Jake knew he had to do better. The last thing he'd wanted was to hurt Cassidy. And he had hurt her. He stood under the hot shower until the water turned cool. He'd certainly made a mess of things.

Tomorrow he would apologize and do better.

"I NEED TO PHONE Harrison," Jake told Cassidy over breakfast the next morning.

She nodded. She still didn't trust herself to speak to Jake without cursing him. How dare he treat her like a lover one moment, a stranger the next? Didn't the man have any respect for her feelings? Did he think he could just snap his fingers, do whatever he damned well pleased, and she would accept it?

Oh, he'd apologized prettily enough, but she'd given him her stiff back. They weren't children. If he didn't want her, fine. But at least have the decency not to toy with her. Why had he kissed her like that if he didn't want to make love to her?

Maybe he can't help himself.

Sure, he can't stop himself from kissing me, but he can stop himself from making love.

You're expecting him to be rational.

So?

You're expecting him to think like we do.

So?

He's a man.

Duh!

And he's confused.

"He's not the only one."

"Talking to yourself again?" Jake asked with a cocked eyebrow.

"It beats the alternative."

"You mean talking to me?" Jake washed his empty cereal bowl in the sink, then set it to drain before turning to her.

Cassidy didn't answer. Instead, she packed her toilet articles, thrusting yesterday's clothes into her backpack without taking the time to fold them.

"You can't ignore me all day, Sunshine."

She could, but it would be childish of her. "Fine. Why do we need to call Harrison? Every time we do, those guys out there catch up with us."

"I've been thinking about it." Jake unlocked the car doors and they both climbed in. He waited until she'd fastened her seat belt before continuing. "The bad guys may have staked out the alumni Internet site on the Web."

"Huh?"

"We have to assume they know we went to the fraternity house and asked questions. If we pull a name and address off the site, they may be able to trace our hit."

"Can we hide our search?"

"Not really. Every computer leaves a signature. And if we use a different computer, they'll still know it's us."

"How?"

"Not many people will be searching out university alumni from thirty years ago. If we hit the site, they'll assume it's us no matter which computer we use."

She stared at the road straight ahead, wondering where they were headed next. "So what do we do?"

"We pull off every fraternity name for every year they've had members. We hit the local registry. Every member in the national registry."

"There'll be so many hits, they won't know which old friend of Michael Scott's we're really after?"

"That's the idea. I should warn you, the deception probably won't work. By now our pursuers have talked to the same people in the fraternity house as we have. They know we're looking for Michael's friends and still might reach them before we do. And we need to trade cars again."

The conversation had been terse, with little byplay between them. No pats of encouragement. No nicknames. She had kept her voice even and businesslike, and he had done the same.

And yet there was a tension between them that hadn't been cleared. A tension Cassidy had no idea how to fix. Maybe she didn't need to fix it. After all, if she stayed mad, there would be no more frustrating kisses, no more wondering where she stood with Jake. No more wondering about whether she had the courage to make him part of her future.

She kept her thoughts to herself as Jake swapped cars and called Harrison. When Jake returned with a list of names and addresses and handed them to her, she scanned the meager list. "I thought about twenty young men lived in the fraternity house each year."

"Those five men are the only ones from thirty years ago who've kept their names and addresses current in the alumni register. Harrison is still searching for addresses on the others. Where do you want to start?"

"Are we going to call first?"

Jake considered her question as he rubbed his chin.

''It would be more convenient if we called. Otherwise we could cross the state and they might not be in.''

Cassidy looked at the short list. ''The man Doc mentioned who was a friend of your dad's, Blake Saunders, is on the list, and he lives just a bit north of here in Jacksonville.''

''Blake was a friend of Michael Scott's. We still don't know for sure if Michael Scott and the man I remember as Steven Cochran are the same person.''

''But since Blake knew Michael, maybe he could fill us in.''

Jake pulled off the highway at the next rest area and used a pay phone to call. He returned and gave her a thumbs-up. ''Blake's wife says her husband should be home by six. She invited us for dinner.''

''But we're strangers.''

''Maybe they knew my folks.''

Cassidy wasn't sure if Jake was pleased because they'd made contact with someone who might have known his father or because they'd been invited to dinner. After the stiff conversation between them all day, he probably looked forward to being in the company of others.

Jake was pushing her away again. And maybe that was for the best. She didn't need to become involved with a man who didn't know his own mind. Or one with so many problems and blanks in his past. Still, when she looked at Jake's handsome profile as he drove, she wondered if he really felt as cool toward her as he'd been acting all day.

BLAKE SAUNDERS LIVED on the intracoastal waterway at Jacksonville Beach. The northern coast of Florida seemed just as warm and humid as the middle region they'd left yesterday. The sun had yet to set and sparkled over the Saunderses' house and out onto the waters beyond. Just twenty yards past their screened pool, barges, sailboats and tugs made their way north and south. A few foolish kids jumped the tug's wake on wake boards.

Although Jake found the view interesting and relaxing and Patty Saunders a fine hostess, he shifted uncomfortably on the patio chair as he sipped his gin and tonic. Patty had said Blake would be home by six, and it was already half past the hour. Jake was checking his watch every two or three minutes. He kept telling himself that if Blake had been delayed, it couldn't be for a reason attached to their visit.

Jake hadn't spotted a tail. He'd swapped the car for another after hitting Orange Park, a little town just south of Jacksonville. Maybe it was his disagreement with Cassidy that had him edgy.

Jake wasn't comfortable with her anger. Especially since she had every right to be angry with him. Even now as she chatted with Patty Saunders, Cassidy treated him coldly. No more shared glances. No touching. No idle chatter.

He should have been pleased. He'd gotten what he wanted. All his feelings were again closed tight in the box. He was back in control. And miserable.

His apology hadn't fixed things between them, and he wasn't sure what would. Sometimes one couldn't go backward in life, no matter how much one wished to. Right now, he didn't know if they could go forward, either.

Jake's thoughts were interrupted when Blake Saunders pulled up to the dock in his fishing boat. After he secured the lines, Saunders nimbly leaped onto the dock and strode toward them, his smile and weathered blue eyes pleasant.

After introductions, Blake sipped his own gin and tonic while Jake took out the pictures he'd found among his mother's things.

When Blake peered at the photo, recognition leaped in his eyes. He pointed to the photo of the man with his arm around the woman. "That's Michael Scott and Mary Lou Ellis. They were going to marry right after graduation."

"You didn't attend the wedding?" Cassidy asked.

Blake frowned. "I don't think I was invited."

"Excuse me, sir—" Jake leaned forward "—but Doc recalled that you and Michael were tight. Isn't it odd that he didn't invite you?"

Blake shrugged. "I got the impression...they were in a hurry. I thought maybe..."

"Maybe what?" Jake tried to control his impatience. But after all these years, he wanted to know about his past. While he had had lots of company in the group homes over the years, most kids there had known way more about their families than he had. In fact, most of the kids kept hoping their real parents would come back for them. It rarely happened, since many parents were in jail or doing drugs. But hope had kept the others going. Jake knew his parents were dead, so finding his sisters had become his hope, his goal.

"I suppose it doesn't matter after all these years." Blake downed the rest of his drink. "And I'm not sure. But I thought maybe Mary Lou was in the family way.''

''Why did you think that?'' Cassidy asked.

Blake held his glass out to Patty for a refill. She didn't seem to mind waiting on her husband and stood to fetch him another drink.

In the meantime, with knowing eyes, Blake studied Jake. ''Does it bother you to consider that you may have been an accident? It shouldn't. Birth control was iffy back then. Not everyone could use the pill.''

''You think Michael Scott was my father?'' Jake asked.

''Don't you? Isn't that why you're here?'' Blake took out a pipe but didn't light it. ''I quit smoking, but I miss having something between my teeth.''

''The man I remember as my father went by the name of Steve Cochran, and he died in a car accident when I was five years old.''

''I'm sorry to hear it. I've never heard of Steve Cochran, but you look too much like Michael not to be his son. It's not just your looks. It's the fire in your eyes, the angle at which you hold your head, and if you don't mind my saying so, the chip on your shoulder. Michael had one, too.''

Jake ignored the remark about the chip on his shoulder. Other things didn't add up. For one, Jake's age. He wasn't old enough to be the baby that Blake thought the couple might have conceived—Jake was too young by two years. Or maybe Blake was mistaken, and Mary Lou hadn't been pregnant at all.

Jake shifted in his chair. ''What else can you tell me about Michael?''

''He was wildly in love with Mary Lou Ellis. I can

still remember his determination to win her. And the girl gave him a hard time. She didn't want to marry.''

''So you're thinking she changed her mind and married Michael when she got pregnant?''

''There's another possibility here,'' Cassidy said softly. Jake knew he wouldn't like what she was about to say and braced himself. ''Maybe your mother never married Michael. Maybe she married Steve. So the man you remember as your father may not be your biological father. And the man in your memories may be a stepdad.''

Stunned at her suggestion, Jake looked out over the water, thinking of possibilities. If Cassidy's version had happened, his biological father could still be alive. Although in all Jake's searching, he'd never found a trace of Steve Cochran. Maybe he should have been looking for Michael Scott.

His head hurt just thinking about the alternatives. After all, it was still an option that Mary Lou Ellis and Michael Scott had changed their names and become Janet and Steven Cochran.

Jake took in a deep breath and released it. He'd come here searching for answers, and now he had more questions than before. And he still hadn't the slightest idea who was after Cassidy and him. Or why.

Over a pleasant dinner of ham, asparagus and creamed rice, Blake told them what he could recall about Michael Scott. Jake found none of the information helpful. College pranks, old dates and fraternity parties, even study habits, didn't have much relevancy to the present. Still he filed away the information, hoping something might be of use. After dinner, Cassidy helped Patty clear the table, then they all drank coffee and ate some wonderful peach cobbler.

As they said their goodbyes, Blake shook Jake's hand. "I just thought of something. There was a woman, a friend of Mary Lou's. Her name was Donna Rodale. You might look her up. Maybe Mary Lou confided her plans to her."

"Thank you for dinner. And the information."

As Jake and Cassidy left the house, Cassidy looked thoughtful. "Donna Rodale was the woman in the yearbook with her arm around Mary Lou. While we were—"

"If she married and changed her name, we may have trouble finding her."

"Oh, I doubt that," Blake interrupted, having overheard them as they walked to the car. "Donna Rodale was a lesbian."

"You're sure?"

"She flaunted her sexual preference. She was one of those rare women in ROTC. She wore her hair short and made no bones about the fact she was ready to fight and die, if necessary, for her country." He shrugged. "Now Mary Lou was a feminine little gal. I always did think she and Donna were a strange pair."

"Thanks again, sir," Jake said. As he escorted Cassidy toward the car, he spied a van parked across the street. It hadn't been there when they'd arrived. All his senses went on alert.

"Jake, while we were in the kitchen—"

"Tell me in a minute."

Something in his peripheral vision glinted.

He'd seen the reflection off a pair of glasses. Now

that he looked more closely, he could see the shadows of two men hunched down in the bushes. Every muscle in his body tensed.

Blake had walked back into his house and shut the front door. Cassidy was about to slide into the car's front seat. If he could place her inside before the men revealed their presence, she would be more protected than out in the open. There was no time to warn her.

A plan hatched in Jake's head. A wild plan, but they didn't have much choice if they didn't want to be taken. He opened the car door for her and pushed the lock button down. "Get in and put on your seat belt, Sunshine."

"I always do," she muttered, then looked at him oddly.

Jake gave a minor shake of his head, but he couldn't guarantee she'd picked up his signal not to argue. And he couldn't warn her of the danger lurking nearby without letting the hiding men know they'd been seen.

Jake started to whistle, hoping he might convince everyone that he was relaxed and unaware of their presence. To put his plan into action, he had to time his movements perfectly.

He didn't get the time he needed. Just as he shut Cassidy's door, the men rushed him, weapons drawn.

Jake spun around, taking them by surprise. He kicked the weapon from the first man's hand, then lunged forward, driving the man backward into his partner. Both his opponents stumbled and fell to the pavement. Jake fell on top of both men, who were unable to fight effectively since he'd forced one to fall on top of the other. Jake used his fists, knees and elbows to land several stunning blows.

In the dim moonlight, Jake saw blood streak down one man's face. "We weren't going to—"

"Who are you guys?" Jake demanded without much hope of receiving an answer. "Why are you following us?"

When the man didn't respond, Jake took advantage of the opportunity he'd created and scooped up the second man's gun. He aimed it at the men. Jake reached into one of the downed men's pocket and pulled out his wallet, hoping he might discover their identities.

Quickly he backed toward the car as he aimed the weapon at them. At least they had the sense not to move.

Cassidy had his door open for him, and as he slipped into his seat, the injured men rolled away from the front of his vehicle, no doubt fearing he'd run them over. Jake wasn't worried about the men on the ground, but about the others he could see in the van. The fight had started and ended within seconds, and the people in the van had yet to react. Jake glanced in the rearview mirror. The guys in the van across the street wore headsets. Disconnecting the apparatus had slowed them down. They'd been unprepared to rush in and help, but the two men in front of him were staggering to their feet and one was still armed.

Once again Jake realized that these men were no ordinary criminals. They operated like pros, as if they worked for the same secret government agency. But he had no time for further speculation. Jake started the engine, threw the car into reverse. Hard.

"Cassidy, hold on."

"Get us out of here."

Jake slammed his foot on the gas, backing the car quickly. He deliberately rammed the van across the street, bracing himself with the steering wheel and praying the seat belt would protect Cassidy from the worst of the collision.

Their car smashed the van from an angle but almost exactly over the van's rear wheels. Windows shattered and tiny pieces of glass flew. Metal screeched and tore.

Before the car had even rocked forward, Jake shifted the car into gear and started away. He took an extra few seconds to aim and fire his gun at one of the van's tires. He didn't want these men coming after them. Jake put a second bullet in another tire, guessing they wouldn't have two spares. That should buy Cassidy and him some getaway time.

He suspected he would have control of the situation for only another minute. He wished he'd had time to search the van and interrogate these men, but he already heard the wail of police sirens in the distance.

Driving away, he pushed the pedal to the floor. "Get down, Sunshine."

"I got the van's license-plate number."

"Good." Relief washed over him that she was okay. She had to be if she'd been thinking clearly enough to realize they could trace the plate.

Now all they had to do was avoid the cops, who would consider their "accident" a hit-and-run. At least no one had been killed—Jake didn't think so, anyway. He'd never checked to see if the men in the van had survived, since the two who'd attacked him were back on their feet and running toward them.

He couldn't think about that now. Their car had two damaged taillights, and within minutes every Duval County policeman would have a description of their car's make and model. They had to ditch it fast, before a cop spotted them.

They couldn't just run; they also had to cover their tracks.

"Jake?"

"Hold on, Sunshine. I've got to think."

"While you were talking to Blake, Patty and I were in the kitchen taking the cobbler out of the oven, and we looked up Donna Rodale's address."

"How?"

"In the Yellow Pages on the Internet."

He hung a right turn, heading for the highway. "Okay."

She should have checked with him first. If their pursuers examined the history on the Saunderses' computer, they would know exactly where he and Cassidy were headed. However, Jake kept his concerns to himself. Cassidy was holding up remarkably well under the circumstances. She'd been trying to help. And she wasn't accustomed to covering her tracks.

"Donna Rodale lives in Boca Raton."

"Okay. We'll have to get there first."

"Is it a race?" Cassidy's voice sounded weak. Jake wanted to stop and check her, but he didn't dare stop driving. Every minute was critical.

He headed north, and when he spied a marina, he pulled through the open gate, shut off the lights and turned to Cassidy. Jake kept the small interior light on and took his first good look at Cassidy.

Blood trickled from her forehead down her temple over her cheek to her chin. Jake started to reach for her when a movement outside the car stopped him.

Now what?

Had their pursuers a third vehicle that Jake hadn't seen? Could they have planted a bug in their car and followed?

Out of the darkness, a man came up and aimed a flashlight into the car.

Chapter Ten

"You folks having some trouble? Want me to call an ambulance or the police?"

Cassidy winced as the bright flashlight shone in her eyes and decided to leave the talking to Jake. He was the master at this cloak-and-dagger business. She wondered what kind of dangers he'd encountered during the past ten years for him to have the skills he had. She imagined his work environment was very different from the clean and bright office where she practiced law and people lived by the rules.

While she'd been terrified of the two men who had come at them out of nowhere, Jake had acted with machinelike efficiency. Not only had he honed his skills to a precision that frightened her, he must have antifreeze in his veins, as well as his heart.

She could see the security guard gazing at Jake with suspicion, the patch on his uniform shiny in the reflection of his flashlight. Jake didn't appear to have a hair out of place. He hadn't even broken a sweat. And she was sure he would concoct some story to get them out of this situation.

"We've had a little problem, and we can't go to

the police," Jake told the man. "Do you have a first-aid kit around? I can pay you for your trouble."

"What kind of problem?" the security guard asked suspiciously.

"We were in an automobile accident."

"You drunk?"

"No, sir. But we're on the run."

"Who's after you?"

"That's the million-dollar question. We'd like to know ourselves. We think whoever is after us has connections with the police."

"I should turn you in...but I won't." Although the man's voice was gruff, Cassidy wasn't surprised when he motioned them with his flashlight. Jake had a way about him that inspired confidence, even from strangers.

"Appreciate it." Jake tried to hand the guard some money, but the man refused with a shake of his head.

"Hide the car behind the shop. And then let's clean the blood from the lady's face and get some ice on the bruise."

She barely recalled banging her head when they'd crashed into the van, but it hurt now that she thought about it. Ice would be welcome. And Jake, a man who didn't trust anyone, seemed willing to take the man at his word.

"Jake, how do you know you can trust him?"

"He's wearing a prison tattoo. It's unlikely he has a great love of the law."

Jake parked and the guard led them to a trailer. The air-conditioning didn't quite keep up with the heat outside. The furniture was dusty, the couch sagged and an open bottle of cheap whiskey led Cassidy to believe the man might have troubles of his own. While the trailer had seen better days, the medical kit the guard handed Jake was well stocked.

She couldn't help wondering what kind of man helped strangers who admitted they were avoiding the police. The guard's face looked hard, his eyes sad. As he picked up a cat and petted it, he didn't seem at all worried about the law.

After washing his hands at the sink, Jake used clean gauze to wash Cassidy's cut, then applied antiseptic cream and a butterfly bandage to her forehead. As his fingers worked efficiently and gently on her flesh, she avoided his gaze, afraid she might see tenderness there and afraid she wouldn't.

Jake peered at her head, admiring his handiwork. "It's not too bad. Head wounds can bleed a lot. You dizzy or nauseous?"

She accepted an ice pack from the guard. "I'll be fine."

"You won't stay fine if you take to the road again in that car." The guard pointed out the obvious.

Jake snapped the first-aid kit closed and handed it back to the guard. "You have any suggestions?"

"Where you headed?" the guard asked, then held up his hand, palm out. "No, don't tell me. I don't want to know." He scratched his bald head a minute. "You could leave here by boat."

"Too slow," Jake told him.

Cassidy recalled Jake's remark about getting to Boca first and wondered at the rush. But she didn't want to ask questions. Because somehow whoever was trailing them would eventually find this place and ask questions. So the less she said that could be repeated, the better. Slowly she was learning to hide her tracks, and she wondered how much she would change before this was all over.

Would she become hard like Jake? Would she become suspicious of everyone? Cassidy hoped not.

Jake peered intently out the window, no doubt reassuring himself they hadn't been followed. "Is there a private airstrip around here with a pilot I could hire?"

"You ain't running drugs?"

"Nope." Jake faced the guard, his arms open wide as if to show he had nothing to hide. "The pilot can check our luggage. We'll be carrying nothing illegal. And I'm willing to pay cash for his trouble."

"Her trouble," the guard corrected. "I know a lady who might help you out if the price is right. I'll call her, then leave you alone. I don't need to hear the arrangements."

As good as his word, the guard dialed, then handed the phone to Jake. Jake thanked him and waited for the trailer door to shut behind the guard before naming their destination and setting a price that included being picked up from the marina and driven to the private airstrip.

The arrangements were made within two minutes. Jake counted out ten hundred-dollar bills and left them on the table under the whiskey bottle for the guard.

Anxious to be moving on, Jake held out a hand to Cassidy. "We're all set. Let's go."

His touch was perfunctory, no different from when he'd bandaged her head. Most likely he feared she might faint on him. But her forehead barely stung, thanks to his ministrations and the ice pack. Still, she appreciated the support.

Jake ditched their smashed-up car in a canal that led to the coastal waterway. The canal had been dredged, and hopefully the car wouldn't be seen when the tide went out.

Fifteen minutes later, the female pilot had escorted them to a small plane and they were in the air. All business, the woman didn't say much, except to demand cash payment up front.

After Jake took care of business, Cassidy slipped into the back seat behind the pilot and gave Jake the copilot's seat. The weather was great, no wind, no stormy weather on radar. The lights from the ground shone clear and bright. But Cassidy had a premonition that they were heading into more trouble than they'd left behind.

She kept it to herself. Jake had enough to do. He'd taken out the wallet he'd confiscated from their pursuers. Inside the wallet he found $210. No identification. No credit cards. No pictures of family.

Jake held the wallet carefully by the edges and wrapped it in an airsickness bag. "Maybe we'll get lucky and get some prints off it."

Cassidy could tell he didn't think that likely, but she admired the fact that he never gave up. Jake's determination would eventually lead them to answers. She just hoped he was happy once he finally learned the truth. There was a restlessness about Jake that she'd like to ease. She wanted him to find a peace that would let him look to his future, instead of always to the past.

The pilot made a slight course correction. "Whatever you say. I won't go in low to avoid radar. That's drug-smuggling territory down there, and we don't want to look suspicious and get searched for the wrong reasons.''

Despite her worries, Cassidy slept, and when she opened her eyes, the plane was landing. The pilot raised the wing flaps and braked until they taxied to a stop.

Jake and Cassidy stepped onto the tarmac as soon as the plane stopped. Cassidy slung her backpack over her shoulder and carried Jake's briefcase with his mother's papers, while he hefted the large duffel with his gear and extra clothing. The duffel must have weighed eighty pounds, yet he walked so quickly she had to hurry to keep up with him.

As soon as they were off the runway, the plane taxied away and lifted into the air, leaving them alone on the small private airfield. On foot, in a strange place, Cassidy felt more vulnerable than she had in a long time. Once again she had the premonition that they were heading into trouble, but the night seemed quiet and the place deserted, its silent line of private planes lined up like headstones in a graveyard.

Out of the darkness, Cassidy heard a car engine start. Sweat broke out on her brow.

There was no place to take cover. She grabbed Jake's arm, her heart pounding with fear. ''Someone's out here.''

Jake had already dropped the duffel by his feet. He shoved her behind him, placing himself between the sound of the car and Cassidy, protecting her with his body.

''How did they find us?'' Cassidy whispered, angry

and bewildered and hoping they wouldn't be gunned down where they stood as a car, headlights off, rolled slowly up to them and stopped.

Jake didn't answer. He'd withdrawn a gun and aimed it at the car. Cassidy peered around Jake. She couldn't see a driver. Couldn't see anyone in the car.

The vehicle's back door opened.

"Get in," a hushed voice ordered.

Jake held his ground. "Who are you?"

"If I wanted you dead, you wouldn't still be breathing. Now get in."

Cassidy wanted to ignore the command. She wanted to keep on walking. But Jake had already picked up his duffel, tossed it inside and prepared to follow.

It occurred to her that she didn't have to stay with Jake. She could just head the other way. But in this cloak-and-dagger world, she was like a baby taking her first steps. She couldn't protect herself or hide. While she hated her vulnerability, hated depending on Jake, she had no other good options if she wanted to stay alive.

With a sigh, she admitted to herself that she didn't want to leave Jake, either. He might be difficult, he might make her furious, but she wanted to be with him. Slowly she followed Jake into the car, feeling as if she were being swallowed whole.

As soon as Cassidy shut the door, the driver, a woman, sat up. "Both of you hunker down. I don't think I was tailed, but they might have an eye on us."

Cassidy frowned. "An eye?"

"Satellite surveillance?" Jake guessed.

"They have telescopes up there that can read the date on a dime from space."

"Who are they?" Jake asked. "And for that matter, who are you? And how did you know where we'd be landing?"

"Your pilot filed a flight plan, so it wasn't hard to find you."

"But how did you know we were on the plane?"

The woman grinned. "Let me introduce myself. I'm Donna Rodale."

The woman they'd flown here to find! As Cassidy gasped in surprise, she could almost hear the chuckle in the woman's voice. Maybe Jake had a clue as to what was going on, but Cassidy felt like Alice in Wonderland after she'd just gone down the rabbit hole.

"I figured since you had the smarts to look me up—"

"How'd you know that?"

"I still keep up with some of my former connections. Since I heard you stopped at the Saunderses' residence, I called there. Patty filled me in on your predicament."

What kind of connections? Cassidy wondered.

"And you decided to help?" Jake asked.

"Your mother saved my life. I owe her. Helping you is my way of paying her back."

Oh, the stories this woman could tell Jake about his family. Cassidy peeked over the seat to see the back of the woman's head. She wore her gray hair in a neat bob like a grandmother, but there was nothing grandmotherly in the steel in her voice as she snapped, "Stay down."

Cassidy wanted to believe that Donna was who she said she was. And that her motives were pure.

"Once Patty told me you were heading my way, I figured you'd take a private plane. It's quick and you can hide your identity. Then I merely made a few phones calls to learn your flight plan. Only two small planes headed this way tonight and the next one is due to land in an hour." Donna drove out of the airport onto a dirt road and turned on her low beams. "I'm glad you got here. Since my house is staked out, I figured I'd better come meet you."

Maybe it was the lack of sleep, but Cassidy was totally confused. Was this woman who she said she was? Or was this a trick to bring them in? If so, she sure had concocted an elaborate story. No. She had to be telling the truth. No one could come up with such a story just so Jake and Cassidy would stay in the car.

"Who's watching your house?" Jake asked.

"The agency, of course," Donna answered as if she expected him to already know that.

Jake's voice rose in surprise. "The CIA?"

"You didn't know?" Amusement filled the woman's voice as she lit a cigarette, careful to keep it below the dash and out of sight of any onlookers.

"I didn't think the CIA used stolen vehicles. Or operated within the U.S.," Jake admitted.

"Or hunted down and tortured U.S. citizens," Cassidy added, still not sure she believed the woman. But it all made a weird kind of sense. The mystery of Jake's parents and their name change, the secret password, the cloak-and-dagger detective work and the efficiency with which they'd been tracked—it all added up to professionals. If not for Jake's expertise, she had no doubt they would have been captured days ago.

Donna puffed on her cigarette, cupping her palm over the butt to hide the glow. "By calling that phone number and giving the password 'blow back,' you made someone at the CIA very nervous. 'Blow back' is a CIA term that means a past operation has gone sour."

"So how is a past operation connected to us?" Jake asked, and Cassidy had to marvel at his one-track mind. In his position, she would have been asking about his parents. Yet Jake had to put the puzzle in the present together first, and he did it with a logical precision that amazed her.

The woman blew smoke rings into the air. "You either know something or have something important that someone wants."

Jake dug out the pictures Cassidy had found in the attic. "Maybe you can shed some light on the subject. Can you tell me the names of these people?"

Still on the grounds of the private airport, Donna parked the car under the trees. She extracted a tiny penlight from her purse and shined it on the pictures. "These two are your parents." She pointed to the man with his arm around the shoulders of the smiling woman.

"What were their names?" Jake asked, and Cassidy heard the anticipation in his voice. Finally he would get some answers.

"Originally, Mary Lou Ellis and Michael Scott. They changed their names when they took an undercover assignment for the agency."

"Changed their names to Janet and Steve—"

"Cochran," Donna finished for him.

"Are you sure? How do you know that?" Cassidy questioned, seeing that Jake was stunned, even though they'd suspected the name change for some time.

"Because I recruited Mary Lou and eventually Michael during their senior year of college." Donna lit a new cigarette from the stub of her last one. She looked at Jake in the rearview mirror. "Your mother was determined to serve her country. She even hired a full-time nanny so she could take dangerous assignments. Michael loved her so much he would have followed her anywhere."

"What about the other people in this picture?" Cassidy asked, taking over as Jake thought through the facts they'd just been given.

Donna pointed to the man standing beside Jake's father. "That's Burak Sansal, our agent in Istanbul. It's essential that you talk to him. Beside him is—"

Gunfire shattered the windshield. Donna slumped in the front seat.

Cassidy ducked, flattening herself instinctively. "Jake, I smell smoke."

Jake tumbled into the front seat. "Donna's cigarette." She heard him stomping on the floor and peeked between the seats. The fire was gone, but the stink of burned carpet lingered. But that wasn't the only smell. The stench of death fused with the coppery scent of blood.

Jake placed two fingers on Donna's neck in search of a pulse. "She's dead."

Cassidy hadn't known Donna for more than half an hour, but the poor woman had been trying to help them. Now she was dead. Two more slugs slammed into the car, but sadness overwhelmed her as Jake shifted Donna's body into the passenger seat and then crawled behind the wheel. "Stay down."

Another bullet pinged off the car's hood. "You stay down, too," Cassidy whispered back.

Jake gunned the engine and hunched as low as he could. "We can't just sit here. That sniper will take us out if we don't get moving."

JAKE HOPED THEY'D LOST the tail during the past two hours. He couldn't be sure. Not if their enemies could track them by satellite. Or they could have placed a homing device in Donna's car. He hadn't had time to search. Nor had he had the opportunity to switch vehicles. Used-car lots didn't tend to be open in the middle of the night.

Close to dawn, Jake stopped in the woods and moved Donna's body with care into the car's trunk. He wished he could do better for his mother's friend, but she'd given her life to save them, and he didn't believe she'd want them to get caught because of her. When they ditched the car two hours later at Miami International Airport, Jake called the authorities about the dead body in the trunk. When he was finished, he took Cassidy's hand. "It's the best we can do for her."

"She was a brave lady." Cassidy, clearly exhausted after their sleepless night, looked to him for answers. "Where're we going now? Won't they be expecting us to fly out?"

Jake grabbed her hand. "That's why we're taking a taxi to the Port of Miami."

"We're taking a ship?" Cassidy walked beside him toward the airport taxi stand.

"The tourist trade to the Bahamas is enormous. From there we can catch a flight to Istanbul."

As tired as she was, Cassidy's mind was still working. "We'll need passports."

"I've got it covered." Jake helped Cassidy into a taxi, and they said nothing more on the way to the port. Cassidy laid her head on his shoulder and closed her eyes, but Jake didn't think she slept.

Her breathing never evened out. And every time a car honked, she jerked. He slung an arm over her shoulder, his mind still working on the information Donna had given them. He no longer questioned the veracity of her statements. Her explanations had made too much sense to doubt them, especially after she'd given her life to tell them.

Jake thought it best to follow up on the one clue she'd given them—the name of the agent in Istanbul who'd also known his parents. So now they had to get out of the country. Usually leaving the United States was easy. It was getting back in that was difficult.

Although Jake had fake passports, he worried that the agents at the Saunderses' house had had the opportunity to search his bag. It was possible the CIA already knew about their aliases and were just waiting to nab them when he tried to use the fake identification.

On the other hand, he didn't think their pursuers wanted to alert security at customs, the airport, and the shipping ports. Jake had the impression this was a covert operation among one sector of the agency, but he couldn't be sure. In retrospect, he wished he'd asked Donna that, but nothing could be done now, except use extreme caution.

Jake considered the boats that made the run to the Bahamas. First there were the large cruise ships. The advantage to being on one of these was that customs never hassled the ship's passengers. The disadvantage was he couldn't count on finding a ship leaving this morning that would have vacancies.

Another alternative were the casino ships that went over to Freeport and returned the next day. But most of those left in the evening, and Jake wanted to leave as soon as possible.

He needed someone who could work with his schedule and decided one of the fishing boats might be best. In clear weather, they could make the Bahamas within hours. So he asked the taxi driver to take him to where tourists and natives hired fishing boats with a crew. Money would make the captain cooperative, and once again Jake was grateful for the cash he kept on hand for emergencies like this.

He was even more grateful for Cassidy's company. He'd never known she could be so strong. The unexpected discovery pleased him, and his feelings of protectiveness for her kicked into overdrive.

She rested her head trustingly on his shoulder, her golden hair spilling onto his chest. With a soft sigh, she snuggled closer, and he breathed in the scent of the soap she'd freshened up with during their last stop. But it wasn't her girl-next-door good looks that called to him so much as her attitude about life.

She didn't complain. She didn't worry out loud.

And she knew when to keep silent, following his lead as if they'd been longtime partners.

She'd even handled their on-again, off-again romance with unusual forthrightness. While he'd hesitated to explore their feelings, she was unafraid. Just knowing how easily they could have died with Donna made Jake realize how foolish he'd been. Life was for living. And trying to protect himself from his growing feelings for Cassidy was like trying to stop the return of the evening tide.

He wanted this woman as he'd never wanted anyone before. Holding back was only hurting himself. And Cassidy.

As Jake paid the taxi driver and nudged Cassidy awake, he searched the dock for a suitable boat and captain. He needed a boat big enough to make the sixty-mile ocean trip, but one small enough that the captain wouldn't insist on taking other passengers.

Rubbing the sleep from her eyes, Cassidy looked at the boats and frowned. "We're going fishing?"

"In a manner of speaking." Jake pulled her close and kissed her forehead. Then he hefted his duffel over his shoulder and escorted Cassidy down the dock.

The water sparkled with sunlight. The light chop made him think the voyage would be a breeze. But after Donna's death, he didn't know if he'd ever stop worrying about Cassidy's safety.

For a moment he considered whether he was being selfish to keep her with him, instead of leaving her here. And then he figured if they remained on the run, they'd both be safer.

Jake hired a captain who was happy to take his

money. The man didn't ask questions, and he offered them the forward cabin. But both Jake and Cassidy stayed on deck, watching the coastline disappear below the horizon until only the deep blue of the Atlantic surrounded them.

It seemed as if they had made their escape, when a Coast Guard patrol boat signaled them to stop.

Chapter Eleven

Cassidy clutched Jake's hand, terrified that the Coast Guard vessel that had hailed their fishing boat was there to take them back to the United States. She'd never realized that Coast Guard boats carried guns on their decks. Or how intimidated she would feel as the big ship hailed them.

Beside her, Jake stood, calmly watching as the ship approached, but he must have sensed the fear in her. "It may be just a routine stop to search for drugs. Hold it together, Sunshine. We don't want to make them suspicious."

"They wouldn't have stopped us if they weren't suspicious." The increasing wind whipped Cassidy's hair in her eyes, and she shoved it aside, annoyed that Jake had read her fear so easily.

"Think of it as a random police stop for drunk drivers late on Friday night."

"It's never happened to me." She was rarely out late on Friday nights. She had never broken the law. Had only had two traffic tickets, which didn't really count. And now she was on the run from the CIA. Just thinking about her situation blew her mind.

"It's okay to show a little nervousness. It's expected," Jake told her as one of the Coast Guard crew threw a line to the captain.

The seas were by no means rough, but large gentle swells made the approach difficult. Cassidy realized that both boats had turned into the wind to match their angles. As the large Coast Guard ship pulled alongside, it blocked the sun. She shivered, partly from the sudden chill, partly from dread.

On the water there was no place to run. Nowhere to hide. And while the fishing-boat captain had willingly accepted Jake's money, Cassidy didn't think he'd lie for them.

It's not like you've done anything illegal.

Donna died because we went to her.

You didn't kill her.

A fine legal distinction. Besides we may be blamed for her murder.

Jake wiped the car of prints before he left it at the airport.

He could have missed one.

Oh, for Pete's sake! No wonder the man can't make up his mind.

Huh?

You clearly aren't cut out to be on the run.

Now, there's something we can agree on.

Don't you think it's time to tell him that you have real feelings for him?

Perhaps it was time to fess up.

Jake looked at her oddly, a smile of affection on his mouth. "Arguing with yourself again?"

"Sorry."

"I find it rather endearing. I only wish…"

"What?"

"That I could listen in."

She suspected that Jake was teasing her to ease her tension, and in truth, she did feel less anxious. Until the Coast Guard crewman placed a ladder over the side of their vessel and climbed aboard. Then her earlier worry came back so hard her stomach ached.

Jake eased Cassidy close enough to the cockpit to hear the conversation. The Coast Guard officer carried a clipboard, and after writing down the name of their vessel, the captain's name and the boat's registration, he looked up, his brows drawn together in a frown. "What are you doing out this far, sir?"

Their captain pulled his cap lower on his forehead. "My guests chartered the boat. They intend to do some fishing in the Bahamas."

The officer frowned harder. "Most folks fly over and rent a boat on the islands."

The captain answered with a bit of surliness. "Hey, I just took their money. I didn't ask their reasons."

The officer's attention turned to Jake and Cassidy. Her mouth went dry with fear, and she hoped she wouldn't have to speak. Jake sat Cassidy on the deck and wrapped her fingers around a teak handhold before leaving her on the deck.

Seeming in no hurry, Jake joined the men in the cockpit. Cassidy admired the ease with which he navigated the maneuver, given the way the boat rose and fell in the swells.

"The lady doesn't like to fly. Is there a problem, Captain? You assured me all your licenses are in order."

"They are."

She should have known Jake would take the offensive. But his reply and manner seemed to put the Coast Guard officer at ease.

The officer shrugged off the implied complaint. "We're making a safety check. I need to see life preservers, flares, a fire extinguisher—"

"I know the drill," the captain complained. "We're not carrying drugs. Search if you like."

The uniformed man's eyes twinkled. "Now you know we can't make a search unless we have reason."

Actually the captain's offer was good enough reason, if Cassidy remembered her maritime law correctly. But she didn't say a word. Her nerves were strung tight enough. If she had to wait through a thorough search, she might start fidgeting.

She suspected the officer knew the law as well as she, probably better. Obviously he wasn't too concerned about drugs, or he would have accepted the captain's offer to do a search. Cassidy might have relaxed, but then she realized that the Coast Guard might not really be searching for drugs. They might be searching for a couple on the CIA's most-wanted list. No, she'd mixed up her agencies. It was the FBI who had a most-wanted list, she recalled from the television show. But the CIA probably had an equivalent list, and she and Jake could be on it.

The captain opened several lockers beneath the seats in the cockpit and gestured to his supplies. "So you're going to make me drag out the same gear your sister ship checked four weeks ago?"

"Afraid so." The man looked up from his list at

Jake. ''While I take care of this, why don't you two dig out some identification for me.''

At his demand, Cassidy's heart danced up her throat. Had they been stopped at random? Or was the officer really searching for fugitives?

Oh, please. You aren't a fugitive.

We might as well be.

Must you exaggerate?

Let's just hope Jake's fake IDs are good enough to pass inspection.

I'd say everything Jake has is good enough to pass inspection.

Now who's exaggerating?

I'm simply stating the truth. After all, we did see the man wet and naked.

As if Cassidy needed that image in her head right now. Jake, all male and very wet, running to rescue her with a gun in his hand. That memory was priceless. And the thought got her through the tense moments where the officer took the fake driver's licenses from Jake and wrote their names on his forms.

And you are going to explain about the lie. Right?

While Cassidy considered telling Jake the truth, the officer stopped writing. But he wasn't done. ''When do you plan on returning to the States?''

Jake winked at the officer, then grinned at Cassidy with a smile that took her breath away. ''Depends on the fishing.''

She wanted to complain that she wasn't a fish. But Jake's little jest on her had relaxed the officer. He gave a copy of his paper to the captain, untied the line that kept the boats together and shoved off.

As Cassidy watched the boat move away, thinking

the man could check their fake ID and turn around any second, she remained tense, her stomach churning. She was unable to relax until she lost sight of the boat on the horizon.

Jake seemed to notice the moment her tension eased. "You look exhausted. Why don't we go below and make use of the captain's bed?"

JAKE EXPECTED TO FALL into the bunk and allow the sea to rock them to sleep. But as he held Cassidy, he was filled with a need so strong he ached to turn to her, capture her lips and take what he'd wanted for so long.

The captain's cabin had a queen-size bed, shelves crammed full of Robert Ludlum paperbacks and a chart table. Cassidy took a seat on the bed and kicked off her shoes. "Jake, there's something I have to tell you."

From her serious expression, he knew she intended for them to have a somber discussion. His stomach clenched. "I'm listening."

She twirled a lock of hair around her finger. "You remember when I told you how I felt about us? I thought we were just friends?"

"As if I could forget."

"I lied."

He met her eyes and saw regret there, but it didn't ease the ache in his heart. "Why did you lie?"

"I lied to myself because I knew it was the one thing that would keep us apart. Back then, I'd feared becoming involved. I feared passion might stop me from attending college and law school the way it had my mother. I was determined not to become emotionally involved with anyone.'' She let out a long sigh. "While my father encouraged me to think this way, I went along with him—especially since I knew you dreamed of having a family, the wife staying home with the kids, and I wanted a career."

"You should have told me the truth." He paused, scowling over what she'd just told him. "So you lied to me about your feelings—"

"To keep you at a distance."

"But you're all grown-up now." He didn't bother to keep the hurt from his tone.

"I still don't want to give up a career I find fulfilling. Besides, I don't want to hurt you again."

"And you're sure about your feelings now?"

"I like you. I care for you. I want to make love with you, see what we have together."

She wasn't saying she loved him, but Jake took what he could get. Just knowing that she cared for him made it impossible for him to resist her. Maybe he would have been stronger and could have waited longer if they weren't together every minute of the day. But his resistance was shattered. It was only a matter of time until he accepted what she offered, consequences be damned.

However, this boat was neither the time nor the place. They should reach Nassau soon, and he didn't want to hurry their first time together. While the rolling seas under them might be fun, he'd rather not be thrown out of the bunk the first time they made love.

Jake lay down and cuddled her against his side, let her use his shoulder for a pillow and enjoyed the simple pleasure of holding her in his arms. Physically she fit him perfectly, her shoulder nestled against his chest, her leg bent and thrown over his thigh, her gorgeous hair tickling his neck.

However, it was the emotional fit that concerned him, since there was nothing simple about the feelings she evoked. He didn't know if he could make love to her and then have her leave him again. While she wouldn't deliberately cause him pain, she might not want what he did. Permanence. But he'd never find out unless he took the first step.

Jake knew her well enough to take her word that she cared for him. While he preferred to think that her ability to fall asleep almost immediately was due to her trust in his skills to protect her rather than sheer exhaustion, he'd always had her trust. She'd always liked him. He wanted more.

In some ways he preferred to go on as they had, not risk his battered heart. Right now, he could still fantasize that they might be perfect together. Just like after he bought a lottery ticket, he could dream of winning. But once those numbers were drawn, the dream ended. Reality hit. And where Cassidy was concerned, dreaming might be preferable to the reality of rejection.

Jake didn't have long to dwell on their situation. He could feel the giant swells change to a hard chop and suspected they were approaching the shore. Gently he woke Cassidy and together they climbed topside.

The Bahamas were low and flat. The turquoise water and sandy white beaches beckoned in every direction. Within half an hour they'd docked in Nassau and said goodbye to the captain. It took two more hours to clear customs in the harbor before Jake hailed a taxi and headed straight for the airport.

"I'm sorry, sir," the airline representative told him, "we have no available seats to London today."

Cassidy's face fell and wearily she shifted her backpack to the counter. "What do you suggest?"

Jake had already learned there were no direct flights from the Bahamas to Istanbul. They'd have to switch planes in Europe. And this was the fourth airline he'd tried in the past hour.

He set his gear by his feet. "How about Paris? Or Amsterdam?"

"We're booked." The woman checked her computer terminal. "I've two first-class seats on a flight to Frankfurt tomorrow morning. Will that do?"

"Sure." Jake paid cash for the tickets, and he and Cassidy headed to the baggage-claim area where they could arrange for ground transportation to a hotel.

Jake studied a bank of advertisements, each with a direct line to a particular hotel. He wanted something nice, someplace out-of-the-way and not too fancy. Somewhere they'd blend in without anyone noticing them.

"How about this one?" Cassidy pointed to a picture of private bungalows that lined a pristine beachfront.

"Looks good." Jake picked up the phone below the picture and was automatically connected.

They lucked out, since the hotel had had a last-minute cancellation. Jake didn't feel like waiting for the limo to drive out to the airport to pick them up, so he rented a car, putting down a huge cash deposit, instead of using a credit card. He knew he'd made the right decision when he saw the traffic.

Cassidy looked around, her eyes bright with interest. "I hate to sound like a complaining American tourist, but this island could really use a few more roads."

"It should be better once we get out of town."

Jake paid attention to his driving, but he was much more interested in Cassidy than taking in the sights. The short nap had refreshed her. She'd tied her hair into a ponytail, applied sunscreen to her face and eagerly looked around from behind dark sunglasses.

Although Jake had been annoyed over their flight delay, he now saw certain advantages to an overnight stop. A shower followed by a midday nap, an afternoon swim, a romantic dinner. Dancing. After-dinner cocktails in the moonlight.

"Jake?"

"Yeah?"

"What are you thinking?"

"Why?"

"You have the strangest expression."

"Really."

"Like you are up to something."

Her perceptiveness didn't bother him, although he had no intention of telling her his thoughts. Instead, he reached over and took her hand. "A rest will do us good."

She peered at him over the top of her sunglasses, her voice provocative. "Is that what you want to do? Rest?"

"Among other things," he replied mildly.

"Be more specific."

"I want to take a cool shower."

"That sounds good," she murmured as she fiddled with the car's inadequate air-conditioning in a futile attempt to squeeze a few more degrees of cold air out. "What else?"

"I thought we'd just relax. Play it by ear." He kept checking the rearview mirror for a tail, a habit now, but didn't spot anyone.

Cassidy noticed. "You think we've been spotted?"

Jake shrugged. "I hope not."

"Good." She leaned back, satisfied, and crossed one leg over the other. "This is one time I don't want to be interrupted."

Jake didn't ask her why. His imagination was already going wild. Was she deliberately making everything sound sexy? Or did it just sound that way to a mind already inflamed with need?

He tried to switch the topic to a more neutral subject. "You ever been here before?"

She shook her head. "What about you?"

"I flew over once for a case. My client wanted me to find the assets her husband had hidden in a bank."

"I thought the banks here are secretive."

"They are. I simply followed the man and photographed a copy of his bank statement, which he carelessly left where I could find it."

Cassidy grinned. "Remind me not to try to hide more secrets from you."

"You have more secrets?" The thought intrigued him. "What kind? You have a hidden bank account? You're secretly a billionaire?"

She laughed. "If I told you, they wouldn't be secrets."

CASSIDY RELAXED in the seat next to Jake. Although she looked forward to a shower and a nap, she was enjoying the scenery. In the Bahamas, the pace was slower even than Florida's. Natives waved to one another and happy children played in the neighborhood streets.

As Jake left the traffic behind, the homes became grander, the landscaping more elaborate. Rain clouds moved in from the ocean. They passed bougainvillea in bloom, swaying palm trees, as well as many other plants she couldn't identify. Tension after the long harrowing night had left her tired, but grateful to be alive.

Jake drove around a long winding bend, and she glimpsed the picture-postcard bungalows from the advertisement at the airport. A wide beach and gentle waves were the backdrop for a dozen cozy cottages that nestled on the sand about a hundred yards beyond the high-water mark.

"The place looks deserted," Cassidy murmured. Gulls flew overhead, but she didn't see anyone on the beach. No one at the oceanside pool. No cleaning people. No tourists. Yet the parking lot was full to capacity. Were they all hiding from the storm about to break? "Is it siesta time?"

Jake drove right past the resort as thunderclouds moved in. "There's a van in the parking lot. And two men wearing headsets."

Fear came rushing back and her stomach churned with acid. "They're waiting for us?"

"Looks like it. I don't want to stay around and find out for sure."

"But how could they have known? We even used fake names."

"The CIA has resources you and I can only guess at. Once we didn't show at the airports, it wouldn't have been hard to check which fishing boats were hired by a couple fitting our descriptions."

"Okay. I can buy that, but how could they know which hotel we picked?"

Jake shrugged and turned on the windshield wipers as a light rain showered them. "Maybe they tapped the phone lines, listening for last-minute reservations."

"That's illegal. And I'm not even sure it's possible."

"It's possible, all right." Jake's tone possessed a grim edge that made her realize the severity of their situation.

Nassau was a small island. There was only one airport, and now that they were known to be on the island, they'd have a difficult time leaving.

Jake drove another five miles, the storm worsening. "I don't think they spotted us. It's likely they have several hotels staked out."

"So where do we hide?"

Jake pulled into a condominium complex and parked so the car couldn't be seen from the highway. "We need to find a place they won't think to search, at least until tomorrow."

They sprinted through the rain into a medium-size building. Families, retirees and tourists, mostly Americans, but some Europeans and natives, too, were hurrying from the beach and pool to avoid the storm. While Cassidy knew they melted right into the group, she had difficulty staying calm. She had to fight the urge to look over her shoulder every few seconds.

Jake took her hand and guided her toward the building manager's office. A tall brown-skinned man with a bald head and two diamonds in his left ear greeted them with a cheerful smile. "And what can I do for you good folks today?"

"We were thinking about leasing a two-bedroom condo with an oceanfront view." Jake shook the man's hand. "I'm Richard Latham and this is my wife, Marie. Do you have anything available?"

The man shook his head. "We have nothing for long-term lease. However I've a sublet ready to go. How soon would you be wanting the place?"

"Can we take a look first?" Jake asked, and Cassidy wondered why he was being so picky. Then she realized that no one would sublet a condominium without looking it over. She bit her lip to hide her nervousness, glad Jake always thought so clearly.

The condo was a corner unit with a lovely balcony, a furnished living room and bedroom with a spectacular glass-walled shower in the bathroom. After a quick inspection, Jake told the man he'd like to sublet on a month-to-month basis. He paid for the first month, included a security deposit up front, and the place was theirs.

After they moved their things from the car to the condo in the rain, Cassidy let Jake claim the shower first. She wanted to wash the grime of travel off her hair and skin, but she wanted to take her time.

She had a lot of thinking to do.

You think too much.

Oh, really.

Yes, really. You could very well be caught tomorrow.

Thanks. I feel so much better now.

Surely not even you can consider wasting what might be your last night of—

Of what?

Life? Freedom? Who knows what those creeps want? But you know what you want.

"What?"

"I didn't say anything," Jake murmured as he entered the living area, his hair still damp, his eyelashes spiked with water droplets. He eyed her with amusement. "Talking to yourself again?"

Heat rose in her cheeks, and she wondered if she was blushing. "I don't mean to be pessimistic, but how are we going to get off the island?"

"By going where they don't expect us."

"And where would that be?"

"Back to the good old U.S. of A."

"I thought we needed to go to—"

"Istanbul. We do. But we won't be flying direct. We can catch a flight back to Miami, Orlando or Atlanta, stay on the plane so we needn't go through customs and then fly to Europe."

"Sounds good." She peered out the window at the storm now in full force. Wind whipped the waves into whitecaps, and she was glad they were no longer at sea. "But aren't they going to watch the airport?"

"They'll be looking for a couple. We'll travel separately." He held up his hand to stop her protest. "And I have several other tricks up my sleeve." He paused, frowning as lightning skipped across the sky and thunder roared, then he smiled. "But you're trying to change the subject. Thinking about our travel arrangements wouldn't make you blush, Sunshine.''

Annoyed that he could see through her so easily, she stood with as much dignity as she could and headed toward the bathroom. ''Did you leave me any hot water?''

His voice turned husky. ''If you get cold, I'll be happy to come in and warm you up.''

She spun around and faced him, her heart pounding. ''Don't make offers you'll regret.''

''I'm all done with regrets, Sunshine.''

''It's about time.'' She shot him her best saucy grin and headed for the shower, hoping that this time he wouldn't change his mind.

Chapter Twelve

For all his waiting, Jake wanted the moment to be perfect. While she showered, he ordered fresh flowers from the condo's gift shop downstairs, telling them he wanted whatever smelled best. He also ordered condoms from the small pharmacy, arranging for the gift shop to deliver them with the flowers. Next he checked to make sure the linens were fresh, drew the blinds against the storm and checked the locks on the doors. He tipped the delivery boy for the flowers and the condoms, setting the flowers on the bedroom dresser in front of a mirror.

He placed his gun within easy reach on the nightstand and tossed his shirt over it so Cassidy wouldn't worry. He placed the birth control within easy reach of the bed and then spent the time pacing. Her skin must have become waterlogged twenty minutes ago.

He was about to knock on the door to see if she was okay when she finally came out, smelling better than the fragrant white blossoms on the dresser.

Her eyes widened, and then she grinned appreciatively and sniffed. "I adore magnolias."

He took her into his arms, gently tipped up her chin. "And I adore you."

"Why thank you, kind sir." She nibbled his lip, wrapped her arms around his neck and drew him closer. "I'm kind of partial to you, too."

Although they weren't the words Jake had hoped to exchange before making love, he wasn't about to quibble. Not when she smelled like fresh vanilla wrapped in sunshine. Not when her skin was as soft as moonlight. Not when every atom in his body hungered for her.

He swept her into his arms and placed her on the bed. He had yet to take off her robe. Swiftly, he remedied that situation. He ached to explore her perfectly shaped breasts, yet he resisted, savoring the sweetness of anticipation.

Outside, the hard rain swelled into a drumbeat that matched his primal mood. He yearned to be inside her.

Not yet.

She reached for the blanket to cover herself. "You're staring."

He smoothed the blanket back. "Just taking a moment to appreciate you."

She blushed at his compliment, her nipples tightening. "I've never thought that we... I feel wanton."

"Nothing wrong with that. Someday I'd like you to swim naked with me in the sunlight. No. In silver starlight to contrast with your hair."

He saw the uncertainty in her eyes war with eagerness to go further. She nervously bit her bottom lip. "Jake...I'm not sure I can give you everything you want."

"Shh. I'll take what I need."

"You mean you'll take what I give you."

"That, too." He drew her closer, whispered into her mouth, his heart beating harder than the rain outside.

She reached for him. "Aren't you taking off *your* pants?"

"Soon."

"That's not fair," she pouted.

And that was when he touched her nipple with his tongue. She arched under him, demanding more. He licked the other nipple. Just a taste, whetting both their appetites before dipping to explore the hollow at her hip, the curve at her side, the indentation of her navel. And all the while he caressed her thighs, enjoying the mixture of tension and craving that surrounded them.

She let out a soft moan and grabbed him. "This is torture, and now it's your turn."

Her hands explored him with more urgency than finesse, heating him until he knew he couldn't wait much longer. Still, he let her take charge, relishing her enjoyment, her enthusiastic participation, her willingness to give and receive in a cycle that kept his senses spiraling.

She started to unfasten his pants, but he placed his hands over hers. "Not yet."

"But—"

"I'm not done exploring."

She tossed her hair over her shoulder. "Neither am I." Boldly, unwilling to wait, she straddled him. "Didn't you ever hear of ladies first?"

He rolled her beneath him with a chuckle. "Sassy

lady. You've got me so hot, you'll deny us both if you persist.''

She sighed and threw her hands over her head. ''Fine. Have me your way.''

''I fully intend to.'' He parted her legs and slid between her thighs, inhaling her feminine scent.

When she understood his intentions, she tried to lurch up, but he held her flat. ''You're so beautiful. I intend to explore every nook and cranny.''

And then he dipped his head and tasted her, and she let out a long breathy moan. Thunder broke overhead. Rain beat a tattoo against the windows, while the woman beneath him bucked and squirmed until she let out a wild shout of release.

He let her recover for a moment and removed his jeans, took a moment to don protection. She watched him wide-eyed as he rolled the condom over himself. ''Next time I want to do that.''

''Next time I'll let you.''

''Jake?''

''Mmm.'' He started to part her legs.

''I've always wanted…''

He stopped and cupped her chin. ''Tell me.''

''You'll think I'm silly.''

''I won't.''

She bit her bottom lip. ''Can I be on top?''

''Whatever you like, Sunshine.'' In one smooth move, he rolled her over him, helped her position her hips, and then she slid down until she surrounded him with heat.

She smiled at him and experimentally rocked her hips. ''This okay?''

''This…is…heaven.'' With his hands free to roam,

he caressed her breasts as she began to move, silkily, slowly, sensuously.

He thought he would die if she didn't speed up. But she seemed quite content to tease him, instinctively sensing when he was about to go over the edge, then holding back at the last moment.

Sweat beaded his brow. His blood boiled. And still she held him trapped in limbo between heaven and ecstasy.

His breath came in huge gulps. He reached between her thighs, urged her faster, harder. And then she took them both over the edge, and he exploded in a powerful rush of sensation that left him dazed, sated and eager to have her all over again.

Jake tightened his arms around Cassidy and gently eased her onto his chest, cradling her head against his shoulder. He ran his fingers over her back, her bottom, her thighs, content to hold her.

"That was good, wasn't it?" she asked huskily.

"The best." And Jake meant it.

She was all he'd ever wanted. And more. These moments of loving her were the highlight of his life. Now that he knew how good it was, better than he'd ever dreamed, he wanted to keep her in his arms and never let her go. But he wondered if she had other ideas....

LOVEMAKING HAD LEFT Cassidy feeling relaxed and in awe of the intimacy they'd shared. Jake had made love to her repeatedly that afternoon and into the late hours of the night. She'd enjoyed their time together so much that she had trouble thinking about the future. She much preferred to dwell on how marvelous

Jake had made her feel. But she still wasn't ready to plan for tomorrow, not when they remained in danger and on the run. She had to keep her thoughts on the business of deceiving their pursuers.

Before their ride to the airport, Jake began the deception by hiring two private detectives to help confuse anyone who might be watching. The following morning, with their bags packed, the four of them left for the airport. Cassidy and the female detective wore bright red wigs, blue jeans and white T-shirts. Jake and the man wore jeans, blue shirts and orange baseball caps pulled low over their eyes.

While the two hired detectives took the front seat in the car, Jake and Cassidy hunkered down low in the back. Heart thumping, Cassidy whispered to Jake. "Did anyone take the bait?"

"There's no need to whisper." Jake used a mirror to peer behind them without giving away his location. "I've spotted two tails. A black van and the guy on the moped."

The hired male detective's eyes flickered to the mirror, then back toward the road. "I see them."

Jake squeezed Cassidy's hand. "Stay cool. Remember your parts, everyone. We want them to follow us."

Although Jake's voice sounded calm, she knew him too well not to recognize his underlying tension. He'd ditched his gun in the ocean, knowing better than to attempt to sneak it onto the airplane, so they were traveling unarmed.

She could see the cords in his neck tighten, heard the vibration in his tone and sensed his worry. Was she about to lose him just after they'd finally made such a powerful emotional connection?

Although she tried to follow Jake's advice, her stomach churned. She wished she had time to explore her newfound feelings for this man, discern what she really thought. But with danger dogging their footsteps, she couldn't think straight.

She and Jake would be most vulnerable when they left the car after the detectives parked at the airport. The airport was crowded, and it took another half hour to navigate the traffic, but it gave Jake a chance to scope out the area. "There's a man with a headset in his ear by the entrance ramp."

"The one reading a newspaper?" the female detective asked.

"He appears to be studying a map."

"I see him." Her companion drove the car toward the parking lot. "How many people do we have to fool?"

Jake ran a hand through his hair. "I don't know. Remember, after you get out of the car, split up. That way half the men will follow one of you, half the other. Ignore each other at the gate. I suspect they won't try to grab you until they see you aren't getting on the plane, after all. They may hassle you, but you've done nothing wrong, so they'll release you once they realize their mistake. But the longer you can fool them, the better our chance of getting away."

Jake checked his watch. "Drive around the parking lot as if you want to find a closer spot. We're ten minutes early."

Cassidy frowned, worried. They had to get away. She didn't want to think about losing Jake, not after what they'd found together last night. "Aren't we playing this kind of tight? Our flight must already be boarding."

"We have time. Remember not to rush or we could draw unwanted attention to ourselves," Jake instructed.

Cassidy leaned over and kissed his forehead, ready to touch him, to feel the warmth of his skin beneath her lips. "What do we do if anyone spots us?"

"Run like hell to the plane."

"Can't they flash some credentials and stop the flight?" Cassidy asked, her stomach cramped with dread. She wasn't sure what the future held for her and Jake, but she wanted a chance to figure it out. And she would. Soon.

"In the United States they could, but this is foreign soil. Most likely they'll let the plane leave, especially since it's heading for New York."

Although Jake had just lied to mislead the detectives who would undoubtedly be questioned if they were stopped—she and Jake were really flying to Atlanta—Cassidy still had doubts about the deception. They were dressed like the detectives to confuse any pursuers. Jake had assured her the CIA wouldn't harm innocent bystanders who happened to look like and dress like Jake and Cassidy, but she wasn't so sure. "Maybe this isn't such a good idea, Jake."

"Hang in there, Sunshine. It's too late to change the plan."

"Okay if I park now?" the detective said.

"Go ahead. Don't forget to lock the car and take the luggage from the trunk."

The man and woman released their seat belts and

got out of the car. The moment the air-conditioning went off, the heat in the car increased. Cassidy had read horror stories of children and animals trapped in vehicles and dying within fifteen minutes in the summer heat.

The detectives moved quickly, but she was sweating by the time the other couple entered the terminal. She started to sit up. Jake pulled her back down. "Not yet. One of the tails still hasn't found a parking spot."

"We're going to cook in here."

"Two more minutes," Jake told her.

She bit her bottom lip. The car had reached sauna-like conditions in just a few minutes. Another hundred and twenty seconds seemed like hours. But finally Jake popped open the door and helped Cassidy out.

"You okay?" he asked with concern in his eyes.

"I'm a little dizzy." The plan was for Cassidy and Jake to also split up. But she didn't know if she could go on alone.

"You need water. You're dehydrated. Can you wait until we reach the plane?"

"I'll try." Cassidy wobbled a little on her feet. "We're supposed to split up, walk into the terminal separately, sit in different aisles on the plane."

"I'm not leaving you." Jake steadied her, then slung his duffel bag and her backpack over his shoulders. "Come on, Sunshine. There may not be air-conditioning inside the terminal, but at least it's out of the sun. And I'll buy you a cola."

"Ice water."

"Anything you like."

Cassidy knew they weren't supposed to call attention to themselves, but she felt weird. Her lips were dry. And she felt weak, as if she was ill. If Jake hadn't helped her, she wouldn't have made it the hundred yards to the terminal. The only thing good about feeling so bad was that her nervousness about being caught had disappeared.

A porter approached to take their bags. Jake pulled out his wallet and gave the man ten bucks. "We're late for our plane and the lady's dehydrated. Can you get us a couple of glasses of water?"

"Yes, sir." The porter grinned and shuffled away.

Cassidy wondered if they'd ever see him again. The man was in no hurry. But then, this was the Bahamas. Hot. Slow-paced.

Jake hurried her through the crowded terminal, and she concentrated on placing one foot in front of the other. She didn't look at the people. She didn't watch for the tails. She simply looked at her feet. So when someone suddenly stopped in front of her, she started to move around him. He moved, too.

Her stomach lurched. Had they been caught? She jerked up her head and stared at a man who grinned at her as he thrust a glass of water at her.

She used both hands to take the paper cup, fearful she didn't have the strength to raise it to her lips. As if sensing her difficulty, Jake put his hands over hers and guided the cup to her mouth. She swallowed. Never had water tasted so good.

"Easy." Jake only let her have a few sips before he took away the cup. "Too much at once isn't good."

He sipped from his own glass and then helped her drink a little more. She felt better, but still dizzy.

Over the loudspeaker it was announced that their flight was making its final boarding. The entrance ramp would pull away in two minutes.

"Come on, Sunshine," Jake coaxed. "Just a little farther and you can rest."

Revived, although unsteady, Cassidy leaned against Jake as he half led, half dragged her toward their gate. She heard shouts behind them. A commotion. Had their ruse been found out?

"Don't look back. Just hand the lady our tickets and let's board the plane."

The shouting behind them increased in volume, but Cassidy couldn't tell if anyone was pursuing them or not. She stepped past the gate and down the boarding ramp, entering a line of latecomers.

Behind them the door shut, blocking anyone from following. Cassidy smiled weakly. "We made it."

"Looks like it. And I don't think anyone spotted which plane we got on."

She took her seat, two rows in front of Jake, sipped her water and strapped on her seat belt. A flight attendant demonstrated safety procedure, and Cassidy tuned out the familiar information.

It's about time you started thinking about last night.

Her conscience had been remarkably quiet for a while, but she knew it had been too good to last.

So what did you think?

About the lovemaking? It was great.

And?

Okay, it was more than great. Jake was terrific, so sensitive, and he satisfied some of my wildest fantasies.

And?

And what? Cassidy was really starting to become annoyed. Why couldn't she just turn her mind off and relax like the other passengers?

And how do you feel about him?

I just told you. This was really too much. She didn't want to analyze every last intimate detail. They'd had a fantastic night together, and they'd probably have more.

Sheesh! You just don't get it, sister.

Don't be so dramatic.

How do you feel about Jake? What's your emotional temperature?

About a 106. Happy now?

What about you? Are you happy?

I guess.

You just spent the night making love to an incredible hunk and all you can say is, I guess?

What do you want from me?

Maybe some thoughts about the future? Maybe some thoughts about commitment?

It's a little difficult to plan that far ahead when I don't know if we'll live through the next twenty-four hours.

Now who's being dramatic? You're avoiding the subject.

So what if I am? Jake and I just met up again. Don't you think it's a little too soon to be thinking about wedding bells?

You're afraid to think about him like that, about any man like that.

Cassidy was about to argue vigorously. But then it hit her that she could be remarkably content to live in the moment. She didn't like to think too much about the future, tending to let each day take its course.

And why do you think that is?

Since you're so smart, why don't you tell me?

Because you need to figure this out for yourself.

Cassidy almost groaned aloud. Maybe I just never met the right man, so I never thought about a future with him.

And maybe you couldn't be the right woman.

What's that supposed to mean?

Maybe you're afraid.

Of Jake? Preposterous.

You're afraid of commitment. Of love.

Disliking where her thoughts led, Cassidy picked up a flight magazine and thumbed through it.

Sure, read the damn magazine and take the easy way out. You won't find any answers there, you know. Avoid the hard questions like you always do.

Enough already. Cassidy shoved the magazine into the seat holder and closed her eyes. She wanted to find the right man, get married and settle down with a bunch of kids. Someday.

Why not today?

We're just a little busy avoiding the CIA today.

Why not tomorrow?

Tomorrow we'll be in Istanbul.

They have weddings in Istanbul.

Very funny. I'll think about it, okay?

And she would. If not for her sake, then for Jake's. She didn't want to hurt him again. Not when she knew how much it hurt to lose someone you loved.

Although Cassidy had never lost a lover that she

cared deeply about, her mother had died when she was only eleven, and that loss had left a huge hole in her life. And then her dad had died, too, leaving Cassidy without any other family.

Suddenly it hit her like a lightning bolt. She didn't want to commit to anyone for fear they would leave her like her mother had left her. Like her father had left her.

About time you figured it out.

Figuring out her reluctance to fall in love was one thing. Overcoming it was another. Cassidy wished she could take back last night. No matter how much she'd enjoyed Jake, she'd had no business making love to him when she didn't know her own feelings.

What the hell had she done?

Chapter Thirteen

The plane ride from Atlanta to London to Istanbul went without a hitch. Jake wished he could say the same for his and Cassidy's relationship. While making love to her had been what he'd wanted, his fear that he'd lost her had escalated. She'd pulled back from him, was careful not to touch him, and she rarely shared her thoughts.

Maybe he could blame her behavior on the lack of sleep. They'd flown through seven time zones and had several hours of layovers between flights. They'd been awake for more hours than his fuzzy mind could calculate and had slept at a hotel before meeting with Burak Sansal the next morning.

Luckily the agent was in the phone book, probably since he no longer worked undercover. However, he still insisted on meeting them in a public place and had named the underground cisterns at nine o'clock.

Jake bought tickets to the subterranean attraction, grateful they accepted dollars, since he hadn't yet had a chance to convert any cash into the local currency. He and Cassidy arrived early and walked down slippery stairs into a dark underground cavern.

Jake took Cassidy's elbow. "Careful. The steps are damp."

"It's kind of spooky."

Jake overheard a tour operator explaining how the Crusaders had built the underground facility to store water for the city more than a thousand years ago. Large columns that held up the ceiling had been stolen from buildings throughout the Mediterranean. A few feet of water still flowed along the cistern's bottom, and fish swam by. But Jake was more concerned with searching for another exit than ogling the sights, just in case the CIA had any operatives on their tail. Although he felt sure they hadn't been followed, he intended to stay cautious, especially since he thought it likely that the CIA would either contact Burak or tail the agent. But hopefully the man knew his spycraft.

Jake saw no other entrance or exit and no tail. But that didn't mean their pursuers weren't there. The boardwalks were crowded with tourists. Guides spoke in many languages. Although colored lights shone on the centuries-old columns, there were a multitude of dark places where someone could hide.

"I wouldn't mind coming back here someday as a real tourist," Cassidy murmured as he hurried her along the walkway.

Jake peered at the variety of columns, all from different architectural periods. "Look for a column where the head is upside down. We're supposed to meet Burak there."

They'd reached the farthest point inside the cistern before the boardwalk looped back when Cassidy pointed. "There she is. How odd that they'd place a woman's head upside down."

"The Crusaders weren't known for their respect for the ancient Greek religions. They looted Greek temples of material to build here." Jake frowned. They'd arrived early, but a man wearing dark Arabic clothing and carrying a cell phone looked up as they approached.

"I am Burak Sansal," he introduced himself, and offered Jake his hand to shake. He kissed Cassidy on the cheek.

"Donna told us you worked with my mother."

"Yes." Burak leaned over the railing and stared into the water. "It would be better if you let the past alone."

"Donna is dead." Jake thought it best to be blunt.

"I am so sorry to hear that. She was a good agent, as was your mother."

Cassidy spoke softly as tourists walked around them. "We're afraid we will be dead, too, if we don't figure out what's going on."

"How can I be of help?" Burak asked.

Jake handed him the pictures from the box Cassidy had found in her father's attic. "Do these pictures have any special meaning to you?"

Burak took his time studying each face in every picture. He paused over the happy one of Jake's parents, then moved on. The next picture showed two strangers, one passing an envelope to the other. Burak's hand trembled as he studied the picture.

"What is it?" Jake asked.

"There are some secrets one never forgets, even

after almost thirty years. Your mother once told me she'd discovered a Russian mole in the CIA.''

''Who?''

''She died before she could tell me his name. But I suspect he is one of the people in these pictures and that he killed your mother to keep his secret. If the mole is still alive, still a double agent, that is the reason Donna was killed. It is why you are being followed.''

Jake had thought he'd long ago gotten over the pain of losing his mother. But now, to hear the reason for her death, that she'd been betrayed by a mole, made him more than angry. While he and his sisters had grown up without their biological families, this traitor had gotten away with murder. And now that the traitor was coming after Cassidy and him, he had to be stopped, so his mother could finally have justice, so his country could rid itself of a spy, so he and Cassidy could be safe.

Jake looked at the old pictures and wished the people in them could talk to him. Burak had been their last lead. They had nowhere else to go. They couldn't go to the CIA. How could he trust anyone in the agency when he had no idea of the mole's identity?

''The people that I recognize in these pictures are dead—all except Ari.''

''Ari?'' Cassidy prodded.

''Ari Ben Goldstein. He was an agent in the Mossad, the Israeli intelligence agency.'' Burak handed the pictures back to Jake. ''He worked closely with your mother. She may have told him her suspicions about the mole's identity.''

Jake carefully put the pictures away. "Do you know where I can find Mr. Goldstein?"

"He still lives in Israel but..."

"But what?"

"You're going to have to sneak into the country."

"Why?" Cassidy asked.

"I still have my sources. Your fake passports have gone out on the wire. Our border patrols and the ever-efficient Israeli patrols will be happy to turn you over to your CIA."

"What do you suggest?" Jake asked.

"You're going to have to trust me."

Cassidy frowned. "And why should we do that?"

Jake answered for Burak. "Because we have no choice. This is his country, and if he wanted us dead, we wouldn't have made it this far."

"You are an astute man, Mr. Cochran. I believe your mother would have been well pleased with her son." Burak walked a few steps with them. "I will make the arrangements. You have money?"

"Yes."

"A weapon?"

"No."

"Return to your hotel. You will be contacted."

Then Burak slipped away into the crowd, leaving Jake and Cassidy alone in a strange city, halfway around the world, dependent on strangers to help them.

THEY RETURNED to the hotel looking like Americans. With the aid of Burak's friends, they left in Arab clothing. Cassidy's hair and all of her face except her eyes were hidden beneath a head covering, a veil and a long flowing robe.

Someone took their pictures and assured them they would have new passports with different names before they left Turkey. A man gave Jake a loaded gun with two extra clips of bullets. In return Jake handed over a wad of cash, and the business transaction was complete. Cassidy hoped they could trust Burak's judgment. She imagined the CIA might offer a reward to anyone for turning them in. Or worse, that one of these people was another double agent.

As usual Jake seemed calm, taking the new people in stride, adapting to the situation as if he'd been born to be a spy. Cassidy had expected Jake to pull back into their former more businesslike arrangement, but Jake had surprised her. He wasn't about to let her forget they'd made love, telling her with his hot looks and intimate glances that he'd like to share more.

Once again she realized that Jake was no longer only a friend, nor was friendship all that he wanted. He wasn't retreating from what they'd found together. She was.

He was pushing her on every level—mental, physical, emotional—and while it made her very aware of him, she didn't know what she wanted. So she'd pulled back until she could decide if she wanted a permanent relationship with a man of Jake's intensity. They were so different. She tended to live in the moment. He planned years into the future. And he'd made it quite clear that he was planning on having her in his future, while she didn't know if she'd ever feel comfortable with him again.

Is that what you want? Comfort?

I don't know what I want.

You owe it to yourself, and to him, to figure it out.

Now isn't the time. We're in a foreign country, about to sneak into another one illegally. I'm wearing foreign clothing, traveling under a fake name.

And what do any of those excuses have to do with your feelings for Jake?

We could die tomorrow. I can't think under this kind of pressure. We're isolated. Alone. We really only have each other to trust.

And who would you rather be here with? Who else can you trust?

No one. Oh, she had friends, neighbors, co-workers, but no one with whom she could share her fears, her needs, her dreams. She'd become so independent that she'd ended up alone. And never had she felt more alone than with Jake right beside her, holding out his hand. It seemed a big decision to reach out and take it.

But she wanted his touch, so she took his hand and clung to him for a moment before forcing herself to let go. They'd been warned not to show any affection in public, as this was not Islamic custom.

She would adapt to the unfamiliar customs and the strange clothing. Until now she'd never realized that in this part of the world, showing one's wrists or ankles was considered provocative. Although Turkey was a modern Islamic country where women had the right to vote, attain an education and divorce their husbands, many followed the old customs. Right now she appreciated the anonymity, as well as protection from the heat, the garb gave her. The loose clothing was cool under the hot sun as she and Jake followed their Arab guides into a car with dark-tinted windows.

They drove through crowded city streets to a busy port. Istanbul was the only city in the world that spanned two continents. Divided by the Bosporus, a body of water that led from the Black Sea to the Mediterranean, the western side of Istanbul was European, the eastern Asian.

The busy port was crowded with cruise ships, merchant liners, fishing boats and ferries. Americans and Europeans mixed among the dark-skinned dark-haired Turks, some of whom wore Western suits and ties, while others wore Arabic garments like their own.

Their car stopped at a ferry that carried vehicles on one level, passengers on another. Cassidy couldn't read the ship's name due to the Cyrillic lettering. One of their guides pressed her new passport into her hand and urged her up the gangplank.

Cassidy's feet seemed rooted to the tarmac as dread washed over her. She had the oddest premonition that once she stepped onto that ferry, her life would be in grave danger. A cloud passing over the sun changed the sparking blue Bosporus waters to a sinister gray. But it was the chill wind and an overly curious gaze from a man standing on the deck that held her still as a statue.

Jake bent his head close to hers and whispered, "What's wrong?"

"Does Burak have anyone on that ship who is supposed to help us?" Cassidy asked.

"I don't think so."

"Well, some man was staring at me."

"Okay. Change of plans." Jake shook hands with

Burak's friends, then escorted Cassidy up the gangplank, where they handed their tickets to a steward.
They entered the ferry, and Jake led her to the nearest
rest room. "Change back into your Western clothes
and wear the red wig."

Cassidy did as he asked, glad Jake trusted her in-
stincts. Another man might have insisted that her premonition and the man showing too much interest were
just products of an overactive imagination.

When she met Jake, he, too, had changed into
slacks and a shirt. He wore a baseball hat over his
forehead. "Let's get off this ship."

There was only one passenger gangplank, but Jake
had spied another one for the crew and supplies. They
took a stairwell down two decks and simply walked
off the ship, ending up back on the dock with their
limited luggage.

Jake hefted his duffel over his shoulder and led her
away from the ship. He cast a seemingly casual eye
over several sailboats available for charter.

While Jake made arrangements with a sailboat captain, Cassidy watched the ferry they were supposed
to have taken slowly leave the dock. First the gang-
ways were pulled in, then the lines cast off. A tug
came alongside and a man jumped off it and onto the
ferry. Cassidy wondered briefly if that was standard
operating procedure, but then Jake called her to inspect a sailboat's cabin with him before finalizing the
deal.

The cabin looked fine, if cramped. A queen-size
bed dominated a tiny room with a ceiling so low Jake
couldn't even stand straight. They had their own sink
and shower and a closet in which to stow their be-

longings. "It's fine, but won't we miss the connection to Mr. Goldstein that Burak set up for us?"

Jake stowed his gear. "We won't take this boat all the way to Israel. We'll stop in Kusadasi—"

"Where's that?"

"Still Turkey, but the Asian side. We can pick up one of the larger ferries there, okay?"

Before Cassidy could reply, a far-off boom thundered across the bow of their sailboat and bounced down the forward hatch. Jake and Cassidy scrambled through the galley and into the cockpit. The source of the explosion was immediately clear.

The ferry they should have taken sat in the middle of the harbor. Flames flared out the windows, and ugly black smoke poured into the sky.

Lifeboats were being lowered, but too slowly. Passengers were jumping into the sea to avoid the flames.

On land people crowded the docks, sirens blared, and Jake grimly took Cassidy into his arms. She shivered, knowing they could have been among those poor souls, hating that they might never know if the explosion had been an accident or something much more sinister. Could someone have wanted them dead so badly they would kill innocent people?

It took hours to rescue the living and retrieve the bodies, more hours before tugs towed the smoking hull away. Cassidy couldn't seem to stop shaking. Although they'd escaped the horror of the explosion, she'd never forget the carnage, the stench, the deaths.

Finally the harbormaster cleared other boats, the cruise ships first, then commercial vessels and finally the pleasure yachts like their sailboat. Their captain set sail at dusk into the Golden Horn, a natural channel. They passed under the Ataturk Bridge and entered the Sea of Marmara, using both motor and sail to navigate through the crowded harbor. Old monuments and the new part of the city with its shopping streets, theaters and large hotels gave the city a quality of solidarity, as if it would stand forever through the centuries. Lights made the spectacular domed Hagia Sophia, Suleymaniye and Blue mosques look like picture postcards, and as dusk fell over the city and onto the water, the Islamic call to prayer could be heard.

As the wind picked up, the sailboat heeled over and the captain, who spoke a little English, instructed Cassidy and Jake on how to trim the sails. When they seemed set on a course, Cassidy went down to the galley to prepare a meal—not that she was hungry, but they needed to keep up their energy.

She found soup, bread, cheese and wine. Jake came down and helped light the stove. The tiny galley seemed homey after the horrible event they'd just witnessed.

"Oh, Jake." Cassidy flung herself into his arms, needing to hold him close. "Did those people die because of us?"

Jake held her fiercely. "We didn't set that fire."

"You know what I mean. Did they die because someone was after us?"

"The CIA doesn't work that way."

"But our mole might."

"It's possible it was an accident."

She believed there was a good chance the mole knew their intention to go to Israel, since that had been the ferry's final destination before heading back through the Greek islands to Turkey. The mole had tracked them to Istanbul. And when the bodies and survivors' names were listed, the mole would know that Jake and Cassidy had survived.

They may have temporarily escaped. But they were by no means safe.

"I'm scared."

Their dinner forgotten, Jake kissed her forehead, her cheeks, her mouth. "We're going to be okay, Sunshine."

"I'm afraid of losing you." She finally admitted her fear to him. She hadn't wanted to feel like this about another person, not ever again. She'd lost her mother, then her father. And the pain had left her drifting like a boat without an anchor. Now she had Jake. He was her anchor, but what would happen if she lost him?

Is this what held her back from loving him? Was this what was confusing her? The thought terrified her so much she almost pushed him away.

But he held her too tightly. "Hey, I'm right here."

If she could help it, she wasn't going to run anymore. Not from her feelings. Not from him. She wondered if she had the ability to change as she wound her arms around his neck and pulled him to her. "You aren't close enough."

"Is that so?"

She peered around his shoulder and looked at the man sailing the boat. He sat beside the tiller, facing forward, an unlit Turkish cigar clamped between his teeth. "Do you think the captain would mind if we tried out our cabin?"

Jake handed the man a plate with bread and cheese

and a glass of wine, then turned back to her. "He should be fine."

Cassidy's heartbeat skyrocketed at the tender gleam in Jake's eyes. Their brush with death today had made her more reckless, bolder. She might still be unsure about the future, but she'd never been so sure of anything in her life than what she wanted right now. Surely she and Jake belonged together. All she wanted was to spend the next few hours proving it to herself. And him.

Making love in the forward cabin was an experience Cassidy would never forget. The bow not only gently bounced up and down, but rolled with each gust of wind. And to top off all that motion, it keeled over on its side at a forty-five-degree angle.

Just taking off each other's clothes became an adventure in exploration and balance and anticipation. Cassidy needed to feel his flesh against hers, needed to hear his heartbeat, needed to kiss the salt spray from his lips to convince herself that she was finally doing the right thing, that Jake was part of her future.

They could easily have died today, and she needed to celebrate that they were unhurt, together, alive. Each caress of his flesh against hers commemorated the occasion and was a celebration of life. Of love.

She pushed away her doubts, knowing she loved this man who had unquestioningly followed her premonition, this man who protected her and sheltered her and cared for her with a gentle ferocity that made her feel good about herself.

As he nuzzled her ear and tiny shimmers of pleasure stoked a fire deep inside, she recognized that the passion they shared was rooted in friendship. She adored Jake Cochran. She respected him. And her heart swelled with the pleasure he gave her as his hands expertly strummed her body and made it sing like a priceless guitar.

As a windy gust sent the boat rolling, Jake's hands steadied her. She looked up at him in the dim cabin light, saw concern for her comfort war with his own unbridled need, and she drew him down between her parted thighs.

"Come with me, Jake," she murmured, already shifting herself to maximize their pleasure.

To keep all doubts at bay, she wanted him to take her hard and swiftly to match the roaring wind in her head, the cresting sea of desire in her heart. Threading her fingers into his hair, she pulled him close, breathed in his masculine scent.

His voice was tight with emotion. "I want you, Sunshine. I can't hold back any longer."

She wrapped her legs around his hips. "I'm right there with you, Jake. I'm ready."

She thought she was prepared for the storm of emotion. Still he stole her breath away. And she went over the edge with him, hurriedly, hungrily, happily.

Chapter Fourteen

Their sailboat arrived too late to catch the Kusadasi ferry to Israel, so they ended up chartering a small plane to fly them to the Egyptian-Israeli border. There they joined a group of Bedouins traveling across the border and entered Israel wearing their Arabic clothing. They took public buses northward and finally holed up in a small hotel just outside Jerusalem.

They'd been lucky to find a room, for it was tourist season. The ancient city was holy to the world's three major religions: Islam, Christianity and Judaism. A modern, thriving and bustling city, with many tourists visiting the ancient sites, Jerusalem welcomed all faiths. Jake and Cassidy could once again look like American tourists without standing out in a crowd.

However, their ability to sneak into the country didn't assuage Jake's concerns. Burak had set up this meeting, but either the Turkish agent had betrayed them or someone had learned of his plans. Worldwide newspaper headlines about the ferry disaster in Istanbul now declared that the explosion had been set by terrorists. So Jake had to assume that someone had infiltrated Burak's group and knew about the coming meeting.

It would be safer to change the meeting place with the Israeli, Ari Ben Goldstein. But Jake had no way to contact the man or change the arrangements. He could do no more to warn him than he could warn his sisters. Although he tried not to worry about his siblings, they popped into his mind all the time. He wished he could assure himself they weren't in danger, that the bodyguards he'd hired had been unnecessary precautions.

Right now he could only be very careful and worry about the immediate danger. Although they'd arrived later than expected, the meeting with Mr. Goldstein was set for the following day in a restaurant within blocks of the Wailing Wall and Dome of the Rock.

He'd repacked his mother's diaries, pictures and certificates in a backpack with other necessary gear. "Ready?"

Cassidy had just stepped out of the hotel bathroom. She'd twisted up her hair, still wet from her shower, and secured it with a few pins. She'd dressed modestly, in a long-sleeved blouse and long skirt, in case they needed to enter any Muslim sites. While it wasn't necessary to cover her head, she'd wrapped a shawl over her hair. Dark sunglasses helped complete her disguise.

Jake opened the door and led her down to the hotel lobby and the taxi stand. "I thought we'd take in the sites, stroll through the Armenian and Jewish Quarters if we have time. But first we need to scope out the restaurant."

He had a few supplies he intended to hide around

the premises, since he suspected he might be searched
by Goldstein on the way into the restaurant tomorrow.
The taxi dropped them in a large square crowded with
tourists speaking Hebrew, Arabic and English. Many
people prayed at the Wailing Wall, one of the holiest
of Jewish sites, where it was believed that Jewish
head priests once talked to God from a nearby temple.

Crowds waited in a long line to visit Dome of the
Rock, the golden domed Mosque on the site where
Muslims believed Muhammad ascended to heaven.
Arabs controlled the crowd, who were subjected to a
metal detector and a search of any handbags before
being allowed to enter the holy site.

Jake turned the other way. The last thing he needed
was a search. Not with what he was carrying.

Once again he considered calling off the meeting
by simply not showing up. Although he intended to
see his mother's killer brought to justice, he didn't
want Cassidy or himself to die. But whoever was after
them wouldn't let them go. They'd proved it by killing Donna and probably blowing up the ferry.

If he and Cassidy ever wanted to stop running and
lead normal lives, they had to discover why the information his mother had left him was so important.
And if that meant attending the meeting, he would
go—only, he intended to have a few surprises of his
own.

Jake found the restaurant without much trouble.
And already he sensed danger. For one thing the facility's cashier and bar were even at street level, but
to reach the dining area, one had to descend a circular
flight of stairs into the basement. The stone walls and

floors here looked as if the Crusaders had built them. However, there was only one entrance.

The tables were glass, the chairs Lucite, foiling his plan to tape a weapon to the table's underside.

A surly waiter ignored them until Jake called him over. Then the dark-haired dark-eyed man introduced himself as Joshua, but acted as if serving customers was beneath him. Something about the waiter's face seemed familiar to Cassidy, but she'd never been to this country before and thought it unlikely they could have met. Jake asked for water three times before the waiter finally brought them a half-filled carafe of lukewarm liquid and one ice cube per glass.

"What do you think?" Cassidy asked as she surveyed the menu.

"I'd prefer a more open spot. Once we come down here, we're as good as trapped."

Her eyes filled with alarm, she reached out and patted his hand. "There have to be some advantages."

"Yeah, all for the enemy."

"Okay. Let's wait until tomorrow and hire someone to bring Mr. Goldstein a note."

"That says what?"

"That the meeting has been compromised, that we need to set another time and location."

"And how will he know the note's from us and not a trap?" Jake shook his head. "This may be our only chance. I don't suppose I could talk you into staying at the hotel, could I?"

He expected her to refuse. But a thoughtful gleam entered her eyes. "Would I be endangering your life by coming with you?"

Jake told her the truth. "Possibly. I can move faster alone. But if you stay at the hotel, you'll be vulnerable and I'll be worried."

Joshua approached with menus and Cassidy peered over hers at Jake. "Then you better arrange for plans B and C because I'm going with you."

JAKE WAS NO CLOSER to having any answers the next morning. They left for the restaurant in sunshine that seemed to mock him. From a bench across the street where he and Cassidy parked themselves to wait, he watched the workers unlock the doors and open the restaurant, and he took a good look at everyone who entered and exited.

When Joshua entered, Cassidy plucked the sleeve of Jake's shirt. "Our waiter's face seems so familiar. Do you recognize him?"

Jake tried to match the face to any of the agents outside the Saunderses' house in Jacksonville. But it had been dark and he'd never gotten a good look at them. He shook his head. "No."

He hadn't slept much last night, worrying about whether he should keep Cassidy with him or ask her to stay behind. In the end she'd made the decision, saying that if she was going to be in danger, she preferred to be with him.

He wished he could take that as a vote of confidence in their relationship, but while they'd advanced from flirtatious glances to kisses to making love, he couldn't read her emotions and was no surer of Cassidy's feelings about him than he'd ever been.

She liked his touch, enjoyed his company, trusted

his judgment, but not once had the word *love* crossed her beautiful lips.

Now was not the time to dwell on their future relationship, and he forced himself to put those personal considerations on hold. Instead, he spoke to her softly. "After we enter the restaurant, go to the ladies' room and retrieve the gun Burak's people gave me. I taped it under the sink yesterday."

Cassidy nodded. "Then I hand it to you under the glass table when the waiter takes our lunch orders."

"Wait until Mr. Goldstein is distracted, because anyone can see your movements through the glass."

"Got it."

Jake had tried to prepare Cassidy for every contingency, but of course that was impossible. Most likely, if anything went wrong, they would have to think fast and run. He had passports and cash and his mother's papers on him. Yesterday he'd mapped out several escape routes, but he hoped running wouldn't be necessary. If they were forced to flee up those stairs, they would have no cover at all until they reached ground level. They'd be targets. Vulnerable.

But his enemy would have the same problem. No cover. No easy places to hide weapons. Only one entrance and exit.

CASSIDY HAD NEVER BEEN so nervous in her life. Jake acted as though they were about to enter a trap. She sat beside him on the bench, watching the minutes tick by on her watch, trying to distract herself with the unfamiliar scents and sights of Jerusalem. But not even the multitude of people speaking many languages or the interesting aromas coming from the cafés could distract her from thinking about Jake. About what they were about to do.

She knew he'd done everything he could think of to ensure her safety, even buying her a bulletproof vest to wear under her blouse. Repeatedly he'd warned her to keep her head down if shooting broke out, telling her a head shot was the likeliest target a trained assassin would choose.

Just the idea of ducking bullets made her fingers tremble, and she held her hands tightly in her lap so Jake wouldn't notice. Not that he'd taken his gaze off the restaurant's open front doors since they'd arrived.

Waiting was the worst part. She desperately wanted to get this meeting over with. Stomach churning, her legs stiff from the inactivity, she broke into a light sweat.

Finally Jake stood. "It's time."

Together they walked into the restaurant. The meeting time had been set early, and they almost had the place to themselves. Cassidy made her trip to the ladies' room, retrieved the gun and placed it in her purse. Since they hadn't been searched, their plot seemed silly. Jake could have walked right in with the weapon, and now she had the unenviable task of slipping him the gun, which she did as she rejoined Jake, not even waiting to be seated at the table.

Joshua ignored them at first. She saw Jake using the delay to study the room once again. Eventually the waiter ushered Jake and Cassidy to a table downstairs, where two gentlemen waited.

Ari Ben Goldstein, a distinguished silver-haired man with a military bearing and sharp blue eyes, introduced himself. "I was a friend of your mother's," he said to Jake. Then he turned to the second man. "This is David Karstairs, a CIA agent."

Jake stiffened as the American agent held out his hand. "It was my understanding that we would meet only with you."

"David is trustworthy," Ari assured him. "I trust him with my life."

Jake finally shook the man's hand. "Let's hope it doesn't come to that."

"We're not all bad guys," David murmured. "However, someone inside our organization is after you. I'm here to help."

Cassidy instinctively liked David, yet wondered if she was being naive. She recalled Donna's senseless death, the deaths of innocent people on the ferry, and shuddered. Lately telling their friends from their enemies had become next to impossible. The killing needed to stop. The secrets needed to be exposed. And Jake's mother had given them the hard evidence to put the traitor behind bars. His mother may have died, but her evidence had lain in Cassidy's father's attic all these years. Cassidy's phone call had alerted the mole that the old evidence against him had been discovered, and the mole had been on their trail ever since.

Cassidy knew that the one person in this room she could count on was Jake. She had no doubts about his loyalty, and that fact bucked up her tattered courage.

"I understand you were supposed to have been traveling on the ferry that exploded in Istanbul," David told them as they all took seats around the table. "You'll be happy to know that Turkish authorities apprehended the man responsible for planting the bomb. Unfortunately before he could name any accomplices, he swallowed poison.''

Another literal dead end.

Jake sipped his water, seemingly in no hurry to show the men the documents. Cassidy hoped she wouldn't have to eat. She couldn't swallow a bite.

Jake thrummed his fingers on the table and spoke to Ari. ''Can you tell me what you and my mother were working on right before she died?''

Ari shook his head. ''Most of the operation is still classified, but I'll tell you what I can.'' He waited until the waiter had delivered menus and departed before speaking. ''Your parents and I were working on a joint CIA-Mossad project. And we suspected a leak on the Israeli side. However, your mother thought the leak came from the CIA. She may have been right. Except for your father and myself, our entire team was killed, including your mother. I helped your father run for his life and take on a new identity to protect himself.''

''He died in a car accident a week after my mother's death,'' Jake told him.

''I'm sorry.'' Ari sighed. ''I heard the CIA-hired attorney separated the children. He even refused to keep the nanny your parents had employed in case someone was able to trace her.''

''So that's why my father didn't tell you anything,'' Cassidy said to Jake. ''He suspected the information could put your life in danger.'' And no doubt that was why her father had encouraged her away from Jake and toward college on the West Coast. Not because he'd disapproved of Jake—he'd simply wanted to keep his daughter safe. Cassidy understood and could forgive him for that. "But why would anyone think someone would come after the children?" she asked.

Ari spread his hands. "I'm not privy to the agency's thinking."

With the end of Ari's explanation, Jake took out the pictures he'd hidden in a backpack. One by one, he handed them to Ari. He saved the one that created Burak's suspicions for last. It was of two men, one handing the other an envelope. "Do you know either of these men?"

David gasped and pointed. "That's Karporoff, a renowned Russian handler in the KGB. He died over twenty years ago, but his exploits are still studied at the academy."

"And the man handing him the envelope?" Jake asked.

David shook his head. Ari looked closely at the picture. "He was in your mother's cell. A traitor, from the looks of this picture."

Cassidy frowned. "Maybe he was on our side. Couldn't he have been a double agent, maybe handing fake material to Karporoff?"

Ari folded his arms across his chest. "If that were so, you wouldn't be on the run."

Jake stared at the face of his mother's killer, his eyes bleak. "What's his name?"

"Max O'Connor was what he went by back then, but in this business we change names as often as we move from country to country," Ari told him matter-of-factly.

At least they now knew the reason they'd been pursued halfway around the world. Max O'Connor was a spy for the former KGB, and he still worked in the CIA. This photograph could brand him a traitor. Cassidy looked with distrust at David.

As if reading her thoughts, he held up his hands. "Hey, I wasn't even born back then. I had no part in the operation."

But David could be working for someone who knew all about the secret Mossad-CIA disaster. Cassidy didn't know what to believe.

The waiter returned and took their drink orders. No one asked for alcohol, but the inefficient Joshua returned with a pitcher of beer.

Jake frowned. "That was supposed to be—"

Joshua flung the pitcher's contents over the photographs and birth certificates and diaries on the table. Cassidy smelled an odd burning, like rotten eggs.

"It's acid!" David yelled, and reached into his suit jacket, probably for a weapon.

As the papers sizzled away under the acid, Joshua lunged for Cassidy. Jake shoved himself between them.

Stunned, Cassidy stumbled back, realizing with dismay that Jake had offered himself as hostage in her place. Horror and terror overwhelmed her. She couldn't lose him, not before she'd told him she loved him.

And she did love him. The warm emotion swelled inside her, warming her like the summer sun, chasing away the icy fear that kept her frozen, taking an edge off the panic. She'd lost her mother. She'd lost her father. She would not lose Jake, too.

But the waiter was holding a gun to Jake's head.

She knew Jake had a gun in his front coat pocket, but he couldn't reach it. Joshua held Jake motionless with one arm around his neck, the gun pressed to his temple with the other. Slowly the two men backed up the steps while the acid sizzled on the table.

"Let him go!" Cassidy walked toward Jake and the gunman. "The evidence is destroyed. You don't need to kill anyone else."

"Stay back!" Jake ordered her.

But Cassidy kept advancing, her arms outstretched. "Please," she implored the gunman, "you can escape faster on your own."

"I need a hostage."

"Take me, instead. You wanted me."

"No, Sunshine!" cried Jake.

"Well, here I am." She still held out her arms, willing Joshua to listen to her.

A shot rang out. Jake and Joshua fell to the ground in a pool of blood. The acrid scent of burned gunpowder singed the air.

"No!" Cassidy screamed, her knees going so weak that she stumbled. Jake couldn't be dead. She couldn't lose him. Tears tightened her throat and sobs racked her as she half stumbled, half crawled toward Jake.

Then Ari was pulling her into his arms, trying to turn her away from the grisly scene. But she made herself watch as David tucked his gun into its holster and pulled a very dead Joshua off Jake.

Jake's eyes were closed. Blood smeared his white shirt. David slapped Jake's face.

Rage surged in Cassidy. "Don't! Don't! Don't hurt him any more! Someone call an ambulance!"

She broke away from Ari, took Jake's head in her

lap and smoothed back his hair, her vision blurry with tears. He was still so warm. He couldn't be dead. He couldn't be gone.

When Jake opened his eyes, she was so startled she almost dropped his head from her lap. She let out a little screech of pleasure.

"You're alive?" Joy flooded her as she ran her hands over his chest, searching for a wound and finding none.

"Easy on my head," Jake murmured.

She ran her fingers over his nape and through his hair. She found no wound, no open cuts, not even a scratch, just one large knot.

David took a seat and patted his brow with a handkerchief. "He must have banged his head on the floor when Joshua fell on top of him."

"You mean after you shot Joshua," Ari corrected. The Israeli's eyes narrowed. "That was a hell of a shot."

"A hell of a chance you took with Jake's life," Cassidy said still unable to believe he was okay. He was alive. And with Joshua dead, they had the rest of their lives ahead of them.

Jake didn't try to get up from the floor, keeping his head in her lap. "David saw an opportunity and took a shot. He may have saved my life."

Ari frowned at the dead body and moved to examine Joshua. "Look at this." Ari pulled a toupee off the man's head. He also removed a glued-on mustache, and suddenly Cassidy recognized the waiter.

"He's the man in the photograph handing the envelope to the spy. I knew he looked familiar. He was younger in the picture, but I'm sure he's the same man.''

As Cassidy cleared up the loose ends, Ari nodded in understanding. "With Joshua dead and the evidence destroyed, you two will be safe to go back to your lives."

Cassidy had no intention of going back to her old life, at least not the one where she lived alone.

Jake spoke to Ari, but he gazed directly into Cassidy's eyes. "Hey, don't rush us. A man could get comfortable right here."

Cassidy continued smoothing his hair off his forehead. "Is that what you want? Comfort?"

Jake's voice turned husky. "What I want...is you."

"That could be arranged." Cassidy smiled through tears of happiness. "I love you, Jake."

"Really?"

"Yes. Really. I love you enough to quit working, stay home and raise your children."

He shook his head. "I won't let you quit lawyering on my account, but the kids sound like a great idea."

"The best idea."

"When we get home, I'm going to call my sisters and invite them to our wedding."

"That's a given. I like having a family. A big family. I want at least four kids," she told him.

"You can have whatever you want," he assured her. "As long as I get you."

Epilogue

Deep in the bowels of a large government building in Washington, a message from Israel passed through the cipher machine. Stamped TOP SECRET, the paper was sealed in an envelope and passed on to a higher authority. Each person who touched the envelope signed his or her name to a voucher.

On the fifteenth floor, a man waited eagerly for the final messenger to depart before ripping open the sealed message and reading two terse sentences:

Files destroyed. Joshua dead.

That particular mission had been accomplished, but at a price. An old colleague had died, but the reader simply shrugged. Everyone was expendable. Everyone was replaceable.

With the originals destroyed, he'd bought himself some time. But he couldn't rest. Not until the two copies Jake Cochran had made and sent to his sisters were also destroyed.

The sisters were proving remarkably resourceful, but they couldn't compete with his resources, his technology. Jake's sisters would be found, the copies destroyed.

If they dared stand in his way, he'd destroy them. Just like all the others...

We hope you enjoyed

THE HIDDEN YEARS,

Book I of Susan Kearney's
new Harlequin Intrigue series,

HIDE AND SEEK.

Please look for Book II,

HIDDEN HEARTS, HI 640 (11/01),

next month.

For a sneak preview of

HIDDEN HEARTS,

turn the page…

Prologue

Alexandra Golden ignored the niggling worry that had shadowed her for several days. Two days ago she'd received a package about her mysterious past, and ever since she'd been fighting not to let it ruin her enjoyment over her latest accomplishment, what she'd worked so hard to achieve.

With deep satisfaction and pride, Alexandra leaned over the finished blueprints of her architectural firm's first skyscraper. The two-hundred-story bank building overlooking the St. John's river in downtown Jacksonville, Florida, would boast majestic views of several bridges, thriving waterfront commerce and a good part of the bustling city. Best of all, it would be the first new construction project by a female architect to be added to Jacksonville's elegant skyline this decade.

As Alexandra smoothed her palm over the graceful lines of the beautiful soaring bank building she would create out of steel, concrete and cool-blue glass, she didn't regret one moment of the hard work she'd done to arrive at this moment. Just mastering the math required to become an architect had almost done her in.

But she'd studied harder than many of her colleagues, took risks to establish her own firm, even stretched her finances to the limit to go after the Benson Bank project.

Along the way, she'd made a friend. Charlotte Benson, heir to the Benson financial empire, had supported Alexandra's firm from the beginning. Charlotte had convinced her mostly male board of directors that a woman architect would help usher in the future. A future where women dropped off their children in day-care centers in the same building where they worked. A future where women who opened their own businesses and sought financing from the bank would feel welcome. A future where widows could come in for investment counseling and trust their stock portfolios to the competent hands of Benson Securities brokers.

So with success at her fingertips, why couldn't Alexandra shake the feeling that something was wrong? She'd always been an optimistic person. She'd had her parents' full support, always had, ever since they'd adopted her, taking her from the foster home to live with them when she was three years old and too young to remember her past. She'd grown up loved and spoiled and encouraged to make her dreams happen. She had no bad memories of her former life and no recollections of a brother named Jake Cochran or the sister who he'd claimed in his recent letter was just a baby when they'd all been separated.

At least Jake had had the good sense not to just show up on her doorstep. The arrival of his letter two days ago would let her prepare gradually for an eventual meeting with him. And she did want to see what

he was like, wondered if he shared her dark hair, olive
complexion and amber-colored eyes.

Jake's message to her had been brief, but warm and
friendly in tone. So she had no reason to feel threatened because the brother she couldn't remember had
sent her a note and a strange assortment of papers in
the mail. She'd skimmed the letter with its strong
handwriting. There'd been no photograph of him, nor
had he said much about himself. Instead, in the ten-
by-fourteen-inch envelope, he'd sent old black-and-
white pictures from their parents' era and a copy of
her mother's diary, along with birth certificates. Alexandra had set the materials aside until she had time
to go through them more carefully.

No reason to worry. So why was she tapping her
short-clipped nails on the blueprints? Why couldn't
she keep her mind on the present? Why did she keep
glancing at the envelope she'd left on the dining-room
table as if it contained a bomb?

The items inside had looked harmless enough. Although she'd never had the time or inclination to
brood about her past, she looked forward to meeting
her siblings. But even if she'd remembered them, she
didn't know if she would have tried to find them.
Unlike many adoptees who yearned to seek out their
genealogical roots, Alexandra had focused on her career and the parents who adored her.

She'd just turned the page of the blueprints to look
at the specs for the site layout and underground util-
ities when a knock came on her apartment door. Leaving the blueprints, she exited her home office, then
walked through the living room to the foyer.

As a single woman who lived alone, she habitually

locked the dead bolt and chained the door after she arrived. Although she'd never had trouble at the apartment complex, she'd received a lot of publicity on the Benson project recently. Her picture had been in the paper and she'd been interviewed on the local television news. While the free promotion could prove a boon to her firm and make it easier to win more projects, she remained cautious of strangers.

"Who is it?"

"Package service, ma'am."

Alexandra's packages were usually delivered to her office. But the one from her brother had come to her home. Perhaps he'd sent another?

Alexandra peered through the peephole. A short middle-aged clean-cut man stood there in an ill-fitting uniform with a clipboard held awkwardly in his meaty hands. No package. Maybe he'd set it on the floor.

Alexandra opened her door but didn't unfasten the chain. "I wasn't expecting anything."

"I'm afraid there's been a mixup, ma'am."

Alexandra frowned. "What kind of mixup?"

"The package we delivered a few days ago isn't yours. If you could return it to me, we can deliver it to its rightful owner."

"Just a minute please."

Alexandra needed to think. She knew that package had her correct address, and she found it highly likely that if this guy was legit, the company would have called first. But she'd received no phone call.

Something was wrong.

Her first thought was to phone the delivery company to check.

"Ma'am, if you could open the door and give me

the package, I can show you the wrong address on the label.''

She knew the address was hers since she'd carefully checked when it arrived. Her second thought was to get the hell out of her apartment.

''I'll be back in a second,'' Alexandra called over her shoulder, knowing the chain might not hold against a determined kick, afraid if she tried to shut the door and throw the dead bolt, he'd jam a foot to prevent her from succeeding.

Heart racing, she sprinted through her living room, scooped the envelope her brother had sent off the dining table, ducked into her office and grabbed the blueprints and her purse.

A loud crash of the front door slamming open and the chain breaking the wood warned her she hadn't another spare nanosecond.

The man had just broken into her apartment!

Sweat slicking down her spine, Alexandra slid across her kitchen tile floor to her back door. As she juggled her belongings, she fumbled to turn the dead bolt.

The lock clicked open just as the deliveryman skidded into her kitchen. ''Hold it right there, lady. I won't hurt you. I just need the package.''

She didn't believe him. And she didn't stop running.

Yanking open the door, she rushed outside onto her two-story terrace.

She never doubted she would get away. Never expected to be caught.

But then she slammed into something hard.

Someone hard.

Strong masculine arms closed around her. Arms way too strong to fight.

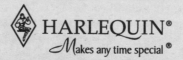

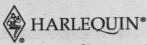

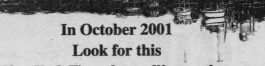

In October 2001
Look for this
New York Times bestselling author

BARBARA DELINSKY

in

Bronze Mystique

The only men in Sasha's life lived between the covers of her bestselling romances. She wrote about passionate, loving heroes, but no such man existed…til Doug Donohue rescued Sasha the night her motorcycle crashed.

AND award-winning Harlequin Intrigue author

GAYLE WILSON

in

Secrets in Silence

This fantastic 2-in-1 collection will be on sale October 2001.

HARLEQUIN®

Makes any time special ®

*H*ugh Blake, soon to become stepfather to the Maitland clan, has produced three high-performing offspring of his own. But at the rate they're going, they're never going to make him a grandpa!

There's *Suzanne*, a work-obsessed CEO whose Christmas spirit could use a little topping up....

And *Thomas*, a lawyer whose ability to hold on to the woman he loves is evaporating by the minute....

And *Diane*, a teacher so dedicated to her teenage students she hasn't noticed she's put her own life on hold.

But there's a Christmas wake-up call in store for the Blake siblings. Love *and* Christmas miracles are in store for all three!

Maitland Maternity Christmas

A collection from three of Harlequin's favorite authors

Muriel Jensen
Judy Christenberry
&Tina Leonard

Look for it in November 2001.